THE UNBREAKABLE SPELL

Rocana Brunt helps her cousin Lady
Caroline to meet secretly the man she
loves. Then Caroline is told she is to
marry the Marquis of Quorn who is in a
tight corner over one of his many
liaisons. Caroline is broken-hearted but
the Marquis, to save himself, wishes to
be married immediately.

Because she loves Caroline and because
she is so unhappy, Rocana agrees to take
her cousin's place at the altar while
Caroline elopes.

How the deception is not discovered until
Rocana and the Marquis reach Paris,
how she finds herself in dangerous
situations and how by a magic,
unbreakable spell she eventually finds
happiness is told in this 339th exciting
romantic tale by Barbara Cartland.

Radio Plays:

THE CAGED BIRD: An episode in the Life of Elizabeth
Empress of Austria. Performed in 1957.

General:

BARBARA CARTLAND'S BOOK OF USELESS
INFORMATION, with a Foreword by The Earl
Mountbatten of Burma.
(In Aid of the United World Colleges)

LOVE AND LOVERS (Picture Book)
THE LIGHT OF LOVE (Prayer Book)

BARBARA CARTLAND'S SCRAPBOOK (in Aid of the Royal
Photographic Museum)
ROMANTIC ROYAL MARRIAGES
BARBARA CARTLAND'S BOOK OF CELEBRITIES
GETTING OLDER, GROWING YOUNGER

Verse:

LINES ON LIFE AND LOVE.

Music:

An Album of Love Songs sung with the Royal
Philharmonic Orchestra.

Film

THE FLAME IS LOVE

The Unbreakable Spell

Barbara Cartland

CORGI BOOKS

THE UNBREAKABLE SPELL

A CORGI BOOK 0 552 12442 7

First publication in Great Britain

PRINTING HISTORY
Corgi edition published 1984

Copyright © Barbara Cartland 1984

This book is set in 10/11 Mallard

Corgi Books are published by
Transworld Publishers Ltd.,
Century House, 61–63 Uxbridge Road,
Ealing, London W5 5SA

Printed and bound in Great Britain by
Hunt Barnard Printing Ltd, Aylesbury, Bucks.

About the Author

Barbara Cartland, the world's most famous romantic novelist, who is also an historian, playwright, lecturer, political speaker and television personality, has now written over 370 books and sold over 370 million over the world.

She has also had many historical works published and has written four autobiographies as well as the biographies of her mother and that of her brother, Ronald Cartland, who was the first Member of Parliament to be killed in the last war. This work has a preface by Sir Winston Churchill and has just been republished with an introduction by Sir Arthur Bryant.

'Love at the Helm', a recent novel, was written with the help and inspiration of the late Admiral of the Fleet, the Earl Mountbatten of Burma. This is being sold for the Mountbatten Memorial Trust.

Miss Cartland in 1978 sang an Album of Love Songs with the Royal Philharmonic Orchestra.

In 1976 by writing twenty-one books, she broke the world record and has continued for the following seven years with 24, 20, 23, 24, 25 and 23. In the Guinness Book of Records she is listed as the world's top-selling author.

In private life Barbara Cartland, who is a Dame of the Order of St. John of Jerusalem, Chairman of the St. John Council in Hertfordshire and Deputy President of the St. John Ambulance Brigade, has fought for better conditions and salaries for Midwives and Nurses.

She has championed the cause for old people, had the law altered regarding gypsies and founded the first

Romany Gypsy camp in the world.

Barbara Cartland is deeply interested in Vitamin Therapy, and is President of the National Association for Health.

Her designs "Decorating with Love" are being sold all over the U.S.A. and the National Home Fashions League made her, in 1981, "Woman of Achievement".

Barbara Cartland's Romances (Book of Cartoons) has been published and seventy-five newspapers in the United States.

Author's Note

A sword-stick is a walking stick which conceals a sharp rapier-like steel blade. Sword sticks date from the 1730s and continued in production until the late 19th century.

In 1820 Calais could be reached from Dover in three hours and the passage even in bad weather rarely took longer than five or six.

Of the public transport available in France the *diligence* was the quickest and the horses, which were changed every twelve miles, travelled at a gallop. There were thirty and a half posts between Calais and Paris.

The only comfortable way however, was for travellers to take their own horses and well – sprung carriages. This was needless to say, very expensive.

CHAPTER ONE

1820

Rocana was sitting sewing in the window-seat of what had been the School-Room of the Castle when the door was burst open.

She looked up to see her cousin and realised at one glance at her lovely face that something was wrong.

"What is it, Caroline?" she asked.

It seemed as if for a moment Lady Caroline Brunt found it impossible to reply.

Then as she walked towards Rocana she said furiously:

"I will not do it! I will not marry him whatever Papa may say!"

"Marry!" Rocana exclaimed. "What are you talking about?"

Caroline sat down on the window-seat and clasping her hands together answered:

"You will not believe what has – happened!"

Rocana put down the lace she was mending with very small stitches which trimmed the Duchess's gown.

"Tell me about it," she said in her soft voice. "I can see it has upset you."

"Upset me!" Caroline exclaimed. "I am furious and completely devastated, but I do not know what to do – about it!"

There was something pathetic in the last words and Rocana bent forward to put her hand on Caroline's.

"Tell me," she begged.

"Papa has just told me that he has invited the

11

Marquis of Quorn to stay for the Steeple Chase that takes place on Wednesday," Caroline replied, "and the Marquis has intimated that he will ask me to marry him!"

"The Marquis of Quorn!" Rocana exclaimed. "Are you sure?"

"Of course I am sure! And when I declined that I have no intention of marrying him, Papa merely said 'I do not wish to argue about it, Caroline, you must talk to your mother'."

Both girls were still, knowing that it was impossible to talk to the Duchess, for if she had made up her mind nothing and nobody would be able to alter it.

There was a silence until Caroline jumped up to say again:

"I will not marry him! I will not! You know that I love Patrick, and he was waiting for an opportunity to approach Papa."

Rocana did not say anything because she had always been certain that Caroline would never be allowed to marry Patrick Fairley.

Their nearest neighbour, the son of a Baronet and a very charming person, there was nothing wrong with him except that the Duchess was extremely ambitious for her daughter and had set her sights very much higher than on a mere country gentleman.

Usually Caroline was quiet and obedient to her mother's wishes, and in every way an exemplary daughter.

Only Rocana knew how much falling in love had changed her, and perhaps for the first time in her life a little of her mother's strong will had become evident in her.

It was not surprising that she had fallen in love with Patrick, a boy she had known all her life, because it was only in the last two months that Caroline had emerged from the School-Room to become a Social Débutante.

Before that no Social life had been organised for her,

and in accordance with normal custom, when the Duke and Duchess entertained she did not join the party, but ate with her cousin and her Governess upstairs.

It was therefore inevitable, since she met Patrick Fairley almost every day when the girls went riding to exercise their horses, that not only would he fall in love with her, but she with him.

Only Rocana realised what was happening and wondered when it was found out what the Duchess would say.

Actually, she did not wonder, she knew only too well.

The Duchess had pushed her husband into every position of authority in the County, and had forced him against his will to take up his hereditary duties at the Palace.

The Duke was an easy-going man who was perfectly content to spend his time in looking after his estate and enjoying himself with his horses and dogs.

His only extravagance was to keep a number of race-horses, which seldom came in first, but gave him the excuse of attending race-meetings, which to his relief did not interest his wife.

It must have been on these occasions, Rocana thought now, that he had become acquainted with the Marquis of Quorn who moved in a very different circle from that of the Duke and Duchess of Bruntwick.

It would have been impossible, even in the depths of the country, not to have heard of the Marquis, who was a close friend of the Prince Regent but at the same time was a very different character from the Bucks and Beaux who surrounded His Royal Highness.

The Marquis was by all accounts not only one of the richest noblemen in the country, but also the most successful at everything he undertook.

Even the Duke could not help extolling his successes on the race-courses, where his horses 'walked off' with every prize.

He was also known to be an exceptional shot and a pugilist who had boxed with 'Gentleman' Jackson and

Mendoza and he had also distinguished himself in the war, receiving several medals for gallantry.

If he was a hero in the stables, he was also whispered about in every Drawing-Room.

Rocana could remember hearing more from the servants than from her Aunt's friends what was not meant for her ears.

Although it did not particularly interest her, she had heard of the Marquis's many love-affairs, some of which had ended in tragedy.

It was said, although it might not be true, that more than one beautiful lady had committed suicide when he left her, while others had pined away with broken hearts.

It was also related that he had fought a number of duels, which he invariably won, with jealous husbands who had 'called him out' to defend their honour.

To Rocana he had become like a fictional character in a book, and although she told herself he was too fantastic to be true she found herself adding up his exploits as if each was a further chapter to what she had already learned about him.

Now to hear that he intended to marry Caroline took her breath away.

When she could speak she asked:

"Do you know the Marquis?"

"I have met him about three times, I suppose," Caroline replied. "Lady Jersey introduced him to me at Almack's, and I was well aware she was doing it out of spite as he had no wish to dance with a débutante!"

"What did you say to him?"

"Nothing, I was too shy," Caroline replied. "Besides, he was scowling because he had no wish to dance, least of all with me!"

"When did you see him again?"

"I cannot remember at which Ball it was. Perhaps the one at Devonshire House."

"What happened then?"

"He came up to speak to Papa about a race-meeting

14

they had attended the day before. There had been an objection over the way one of the horses had run or something tiresome like that."

"Go on," Rocana prompted.

"When they had talked for sometime, Papa said: 'You have met my daughter Caroline?'

"The Marquis bowed and I curtsied, and he said: 'We danced together at Almack's.'

"I was surprised he remembered and I said: 'Yes,' and he did not speak to me again."

"What happened the next time?"

"He had to talk to me then because I was sitting next to him at dinner, but he did not say much because he was engaged in conversation with the lady on his other side, who was certainly not going to allow me to capture his attention if she could help it!"

Caroline paused. Then she added:

"He is stuck up, full of his own importance, condescending, and if you want the truth, I dislike him!"

"Then how can you marry him?" Rocana asked.

"I cannot do it! I cannot!" Caroline cried. "I know this is all Mama's doing! If she could not find a Prince or a Duke for me, then a Marquis was the next best thing!"

Rocana thought privately that from what she had heard the Marquis was far more important than any Duke.

But she could understand that Caroline would feel helpless and inevitably miserable with a man who was over-bearing and had a reputation like the Marquis's.

At the same time he might well be looking for a wife, because sooner or later he must have an heir to inherit his title, his wealth and his vast possessions.

Although Rocana had not seen any of the other débutantes she could not believe that any of them could be more beautiful than Caroline.

Her cousin in fact typified the traditional 'English Rose'.

She had a perfect pink-and-white skin, large, rather

15

pale blue eyes and fair hair which any poet would describe as 'the gold of ripening corn'.

She was graceful, she was usually very sweet-tempered, and it was too much to ask that on top of all these attributes she should be very intelligent as well.

When they had their lessons together it was Rocana who always outstripped anything their Governess could teach her on any particular subject, and had therefore had to carry on where they left off and educate herself.

When she had first come to live at the Castle after her parents' death, she had thought it was a prison in which she was incarcerated for life, and she was so miserable that she thought she must die.

Then she discovered the huge Library which had awoken her interest and made her feel she had something to live for.

It was her mother who had taught her from when she was very small to be curious to the point where she wanted to learn more about anything she heard being talked about.

It was her mother who had taught her French, which was her own native language, and had made her aware that marvellous though the British thought themselves, there were other countries and other people in other parts of the world.

"You have to be broad-minded, my darling," she said. "The more you learn and the more you study, the more you will be able to see other people's points of view, and understand their feelings as well as your own."

It was something it had been very hard to do during the war when because the English were fighting against her mother's native country, not only many of their so-called friends ostracised her, but also her husband's nearest relatives.

It was a long time later after she had come to live at the Castle that Rocana realised, although it seemed incredible, that the Duke had actually been jealous of his younger brother, and the Duchess of her mother.

As was usual in the great aristocratic families of England, the eldest son had everything.

The Duke of Bruntwick had his title, the Castle and a huge estate, while his younger brother had a small allowance which meant he was continually in debt.

Because everybody loved 'Lord Leo', as he was always known, although he had been christened 'Leopold', he was welcomed wherever he went, and his real friends accepted his French wife for his sake.

It was however very difficult, as Rocana realised, for her mother who adored her husband and had no wish to embarrass him.

She had been the daughter of the French Ambassador to England during the Armistice of 1802.

Lord Leo had seen her at a party in London, and had immediately known she was what he had been looking for all his life.

Very good-looking, popular, a man's man, though at the same time women were wildly attracted to him, 'Lord Leo' had a charm which few people and no animal could resist.

If he had fallen in love with Yvette de Soissons, it was not surprising that she had fallen in love with him.

In spite of the disapproval of the Duke and Duchess of Bruntwick and the anxious concern of the Ambassador, they were married within a few months.

To say they were happy was to put it mildly.

They were ecstatic and everything was perfect until hostilities broke out again between Britain and France.

The Ambassador returned to Paris, and although he was a rich man he was unable to send his daughter any money.

"I am just an encumbrance!" Rocana heard her mother say once when she did not know she was listening.

"What do I want with money?" her father asked, "when you have given me the moon, the stars and a

17

happiness which Midas himself could not exceed?"

He had swept her into his arms and kissed her until they were laughing because it was so wonderful to be together, and Rocana had known from that moment that money could not buy love.

She was made aware as soon as she came to the Castle that she was an object of contempt.

Seldom a day passed that the Duchess did not point out that she was not only an orphan, but a penniless one, and that she had to be grateful to her Uncle not only for a roof over her head, but for every crumb of food she put into her mouth.

"Extravagant, irresponsible and utterly improvident, that is what your father was!" she would say contemptibly "As for your mother . . .!"

There was no need for words for the Duchess to describe what she thought of her dead sister-in-law.

When Rocana looked in the mirror and knew she resembled her mother she realised why the Duchess hated them both.

The Duke of course, had made an arranged marriage, as was usual, and as it was the merger of two great families, it had been considered very commendable.

The Duchess's father, the Duke of Hull, had given her a very large dowry and on his death she had inherited several Squares and Streets in London, the rents of which every year came to quite a considerable sum.

She had given the Duke the heir he desired, and had intrigued until he was appointed Master of the Horse to the King, a position in which at the moment he had little to do since the Monarch was dying.

The Duchess then produced Caroline, some years later who fortunately took after her father and inherited the good looks of his family.

There had been beautiful Duchesses of Bruntwick all down the centuries, and yet because her mother was so lovely Rocana had managed to combine the beauty of both her English and her French Ancestors

18

in a manner which made her unique.

It also resulted in her being kept by her Aunt from taking any part in family social activities from the time she left the School-Room.

As she was nearly a year older than Caroline, this meant their companionship was confined to their bedrooms and the School-Room, and unless the family were alone Rocana did not go downstairs for meals.

At first she could hardly believe that her Aunt really intended to isolate her in such a way, and thought perhaps she was just prolonging her mourning for her father, who had died a year after her mother.

Then the Duchess had spelt it out to her very simply:

"I never approved of your father, Rocana," she said in her sharp voice, "and as you know, your mother was an enemy of this country, an alien, who should in my opinion have been imprisoned while we were at war. I therefore have no wish for you to meet Caroline's friends, or impose on her when we are entertaining."

She paused before she went on spitefully:

"You can try to make yourself more useful than you are at the moment by helping with her gowns and tidying her room when the housemaids are busy. When we go to London, you will of course stay here!"

It had taken Caroline's old Nanny to make it clear to Rocana why she was being treated in such a way.

"Now don't upset yourself, dearie," she said when she found Rocana in tears. "Her Grace's just jealous, and there's no other word for it."

"Jealous?" Rocana asked incredulously.

"She always was plain, even when she was young, and now with lines on her face and a stout figure you could hardly expect her not to see the difference between herself and your mother!"

"I never thought of her being jealous of Mama!"

"Of course she was jealous!" Nanny said sharply. "Just as His Grace was jealous of Lord Leo. How could he help it when everybody loved your father? He rode better than His Grace, and always beat him in any

Steeple-Chase or Point-to-Point, even when they was young boys!"

Rocana had stood in front of the mirror and realised that while she had fair hair, which was characteristic of the Bruntwicks, her eyes, because her mother was dark, were not blue like Caroline's but a strange colour that in certain lights seemed almost purple.

"Pansy eyes," her father called them and told her mother that hers hypnotised him so that he could never escape from them.

They certainly were strange, Rocana thought, against her pink-and-white complexion, which again was part of the Bruntwick tradition.

But her face was heart-shaped which she had seen in so many portraits of her French ancestors and when she smiled she had a mischievous twist to her lips which was unlike the perfect Cupid bow in Caroline's face.

She remembered her father saying to her mother once:

"I think, my darling, you are a witch. You have certainly bewitched me! Perhaps you are the re-incarnation of Morgan le Fay, or one of the mediaeval witches who were burned at the stake because the people were frightened of them!"

"Are you frightened of me?" her mother asked softly.

"Only frightened of losing you," her father replied, "and you know as well as I do that a man has only to look at you to find you irresistible!"

Her mother had laughed and said:

"If they do it is only a compliment to you, my darling. As far as I am concerned there is only one man in the whole world, and I shall use every spell I know to keep him captive!"

As if she was following her thoughts Nanny standing behind Rocana said:

"You're too pretty, and that's the truth! And I often find myself wondering since Her Grace never lets you meet anybody where you'll find yourself a husband!''

It was a dismal thought, because when she passed her eighteenth birthday Rocana knew she would like to be married, if only to escape from the Castle.

Of course she dreamt of finding a Knight in Shining Armour or a Prince looking exactly like her father, who would fall in love with her at first sight and carry her away on his Charger.

But she had known ever since she had come to the Castle that the reason why she was unhappy there was not only that her Aunt disliked her, but also that it was a house without love.

When she lived with her father and mother in the small Manor on the estate which the Duke had condescendingly given his brother, it had always been filled with sunshine and happiness.

Her father and mother had given it a warmth which had nothing to do with the big log fires that burned in the open fireplaces.

But in the Castle, even in the height of summer, Rocana always found herself shivering.

When Caroline had gone to London this April, excited by the lovely gowns that had been given to her for the Balls, and anticipating that she would be a success, Rocana left behind, felt very lonely.

Then she told herself it was no use crying for the moon. She must just be grateful for the few pleasures that were left to her.

These consisted mainly of the horses she was allowed to ride, though that was often impossible when the Duchess found her a great deal of sewing to do, and the books she could read.

This usually had to be at night, often until the early hours of the morning, because she had been kept so busy in the daytime.

She was never accompanied when she went riding because the Duke thought it was a waste of time to send a groom with either her or Caroline when they rode just around the Castle grounds.

It was inevitable that Patrick Fairley was waiting for her, distraught in case when she reached London Caroline would forget him.

"Do you think Caroline loves me, Rocana?" he would ask her over and over again. "I mean – really loves me? Or that she remembers she belongs to me?"

Rocana tried to console him, for she was sure that Caroline loved him as much as she was capable of loving anybody.

It was not that ecstatic, rapturous love that her mother had had for her father, but then she doubted if anybody as wholly English as Caroline would be able to feel like that.

When Caroline returned to the Castle in the middle of June when the Prince Regent had left London for Brighton and the Season was over, there was no doubt that she was delighted to see Patrick.

Every morning she would ride with Rocana across the Park, through the woods in the direction of Patrick's much smaller estate which marched with the Duke's, and he would meet them half-way.

Rocana would then tactfully ride off on her own and would leave them until it was time to return home.

She would not have been human if sometimes she did not long for somebody to look at her with loving eyes as Patrick looked at Caroline, and to hear the deep note in his voice which was very different from when he spoke to her.

'Perhaps I shall just grow old, never meeting anybody and never going anywhere,' she thought sometimes despairingly.

She tried to lose herself in her dreams and in the books that she took down one after another from the shelves of the Library which otherwise remained undisturbed, year after year.

She knew now, however, that whatever Caroline might say, however much she loved Patrick, she would be forced to marry the Marquis of Quorn, and perhaps she would find him, if nothing else, a very exciting husband.

"What am I to do, Rocana?" Caroline was asking desperately. "I have to marry Patrick! You know I have to! Anyway, I could never cope with a man like the Marquis, even if I liked him!"

Rocana thought that was undoubtedly true, and she asked:

"What is he like? Describe him to me."

"I suppose he is handsome," Caroline said reluctantly, "but he is overpowering, overwhelming, and the other girls in London all whispered about him and his love-affairs."

"And told you about them?" Rocana asked.

"Of course they did," Caroline replied. "Nobody in London talks of anything but love, and they were always saying how some woman was weeping because the Marquis had left her or another really was crowing her head off because he had transferred his affections to her."

It was what Rocana had already heard from the servants and she said:

"Why do you think he wants to be married?"

"I know the answer to that."

"You do?"

"Yes, he is in a mess with some Diplomat's wife and he is trying to escape from what might cause an international incident."

"Are you saying," Rocana asked incredueously, "that that is why he is proposing to marry you?"

Caroline sat down on the window-seat.

"When I arrived in London everyone talked about the Marquis – they never seemed interested in anybody else. They said he was determined never to marry because to live with one woman would bore him in a week and he preferred having a whole pack of them like fox-hounds!"

"I think that sounds horrid!" Rocana exclaimed.

"That is what I thought," Caroline agreed, "but I was not really interested in him because I was thinking of Patrick."

"Yes, of course! Go on!"

"Then they began to talk about this 'Madame something or other' – I cannot remember her name – and how beautiful she was with red hair and green eyes, and they whispered and whispered as to what she and the Marquis were doing together."

"Then what happened?"

"I came home, and today Papa has told me the Marquis is coming to stay and that when they met at Royal Ascot he had intimated that he might pay his addresses to me."

"Might?" Rocana questioned.

"I suppose he did not wish to commit himself in case his difficulty turned out to be not as awkward as he thought," Caroline said bitterly.

Because she seemed to have grasped the situation far more clearly than Rocana would have expected her to do, she merely stared at her cousin as she said:

"I think the way he is behaving is insulting and your father should have refused."

"I think Papa would, if I asked him to do so," Caroline replied. "But you know Mama would prevent him from doing anything but accept the Marquis with alacrity, and she will never, never let me say 'No'."

As this was the truth, Rocana did not argue. She merely said sympathetically:

"Oh, Caroline, I am so sorry for you."

"What can I do, Rocana? I must tell Patrick, and ask his advice."

"You will have to wait until tomorrow morning."

"I cannot! I cannot wait as long as that! I have to see him this evening!"

She gave a little cry.

"I can do that, as Mama and Papa are going to dinner with the High Sheriff and I have not been included in the invitation."

She looked at Rocana and said:

"This is where you have to help me, dearest. You must ride over to the Grange and tell Patrick he is to meet me at our usual place. He had better not come here in case one of the servants tells Mama."

"No, of course not," Rocana said, "but how shall we explain my absence if Aunt Sophie asks for me?"

"Do you think she is likely to do that?"

Rocana made a little gesture with her hands before she said:

"She might easily suspect I am saying something to you about your wedding which I ought not to and so come in here to stop it."

Caroline knew this was just the way her mother would think and she got up and walked restlessly about the room.

"I must see Patrick, I must!" she said.

"I will go and fetch him," Rocana said, "but I had better wait until after five o'clock when your mother will be resting. You had better go and sit with her and keep her talking about the Marquis."

Caroline made a little grimace, but she knew Rocana was talking sense, and she agreed that it was the only way they could escape detection.

They went on talking, with Caroline saying over and over again that she could not marry anybody but Patrick.

Rocana was aware that her cousin knew she was fighting a losing battle.

Unless a miracle occurred when the Marquis arrived the day after tomorrow, she would be forced to accept his proposal and there would be no escape.

. . . .

As Rocana rode through the fields, enjoying although she thought it was selfish of her, being able to get away from the Castle and the large amount of sewing she was forced to do, she was aware that she was going on an ill-fated errand.

However much Patrick might love Caroline or she him, there was no possible way in which his offer of marriage could compare with that of the Marquis of Quorn.

In fact she was quite certain that in the circumstances both the Duke and the Duchess would treat it as merely an impertinence.

Knowing Caroline as well as she did she was aware that while she would make Patrick an excellent wife and they would undoubtedly be very happy, she would never in a million years be able to find happiness with somebody like the Marquis.

Because she had heard so much about him, to Rocana he was half-satyr and half-rake, and she thought that only the lady with the red hair and green eyes was likely to prove the type of wife he should have to keep him in order.

Knowing so little of the Social World, she thought it was only love which would make a man like that happy, and keep him faithful to one woman.

She was well aware that her father had had a great number of love-affairs before he met her mother. It was in fact, inevitable when he was so attractive and enjoyed life so tremendously.

Lord Leo did not envy his brother his vast wealth, his Castle, his estates and his superlative horses.

He just laughed at poverty as he laughed at everything else and made the best of what horses he had, riding them so superbly that it was he who won the race rather than the horse.

Because he brought the joy of living to everybody with whom he came in contact it was inevitable, as her mother had said jokingly, that women should follow him as if he was the 'Pied Piper'.

"When I met you, my darling," her father had said, "they all vanished, just as the rats did, never to return!"

Her mother had laughed.

"Can I be sure of that?"

"As you are a witch," her father replied, "you know I am tied to you by a spell I cannot break and an enchantment which I could not bear to lose."

Thinking of how much they had meant to each other,

Rocana thought that perhaps that was what the Marquis needed, an enchantment from which he would find no way of escape nor have any wish to do so.

She was aware that, sweet and gentle and kind though Caroline was, that was something she would be unable to give him.

Rocana was certain that soon after they were married he would go back to the Siren with the red hair and green eyes, and Caroline would sit lonely at home.

It was the sort of life she had heard so many wives of aristocrats were forced to live while their husbands had what was called 'other interests'.

They were whispered about in Drawing-Rooms as well as in kitchens and stables, in fact everywhere where gossips congregated.

"How can I save her?" Rocana asked, and knew there was no answer to that.

. . . .

Rocana reached the boundary of the Duke's estate where it marched with the Fairleys' and began to look around her hoping perhaps she would see Patrick in the distance.

He not only trained a number of horses for his father, but also supervised the workers on the estate, intending when he took over to manage it himself, rather than employ somebody to do it for him.

It was the sort of thing her father would have enjoyed, Rocana knew, if he had only had enough money and enough acres of his own to farm.

But the Duke had only given him the Manor and a few surrounding fields, and he had often found time heavy on his hands.

This had tempted him and her mother to go off to London and spend money they could not afford enjoying themselves.

"I suppose it is important to everybody to be kept busy, to keep them out of mischief," Rocana thought philosophically.

Then she remembered with a little sigh how much work the Duchess had given her to do which at the moment was lying neglected in the Castle.

She had almost reached the Grange, which though not a great house was quite imposing and attractive with its mellow red brick, when with a feeling of relief she saw Patrick come out of the wood to her right, and knew that he was going home.

She spurred her horse and as she galloped towards him, he recognised her and came to meet her.

As their horses drew alongside each other, he exclaimed:

"Rocana! What are you doing here?"

"I have come to tell you," Rocana replied breathlessly, "that Caroline wants to see you immediately, and it is very, very important!"

"What has happened?"

Rocana knew that Patrick was quick-witted and she saw the concern in his eyes, which told her he was already anticipating what was wrong.

"I think Caroline would rather tell you herself."

She turned her horse back in the direction she had come and Patrick rode beside her.

"Please tell me, Rocana," he said. "If it is what I fear, it will give me time to think out what I should say."

Rocana realised he was talking sense.

"Caroline is distraught and miserable," she said, "because the Duke has told her that the Marquis of Quorn is coming to stay and intends to ask her to marry him."

She heard Patrick give a gasp. Then he said:

"The Marquis of Quorn? It cannot be true!"

"It is!"

"How can she possibly marry a man . . .?"

He stopped. Then in a different tone of voice he said more quietly:

"This is what I feared might happen if she went to London, but I never anticipated her marrying the Marquis – of all people!"

28

"I feel the same," Rocana replied, "but you know it is the sort of marriage the Duchess will want for her."

"Of course," Patrick said, "although doubtless Her Grace would have preferred the Prince Regent, if he were not already married!"

Patrick's tone was very bitter and Rocana said quickly:

"Try not to make Caroline more distressed than she is already. You know she loves you."

"And I love her!" Patrick said. "But I have as much chance of marrying her as flying to the moon!"

There was silence and they rode for a little way before Rocana said:

"I think perhaps you are rather faint-hearted to give up so easily!"

Patrick looked at her sharply.

"What do you mean by that?"

"In fairy-stories the Prince climbs the highest mountain, dives down into the sea, or kills the dragon to save the woman he loves."

"That is, as you say, in fairy-stories."

Then in a different tone Patrick asked:

"You said 'save'. Are you implying that I ought to save Caroline?"

"You can answer that question for yourself," Rocana replied. "From all I have heard of the Marquis of Quorn, I should have thought nobody could be a more unsuitable husband for her!"

"You are right! Of course you are right!" Patrick said. "But what can I do? How can I save her?"

Rocana smiled. Then she said:

"That is something you must decide yourself. You know my father married my mother against the wishes of the Duke, the Duchess and the entire Bruntwick family."

She paused before she went on:

"Mama's own father the Ambassador, who I always suspected disliked the English as much as the rest of his compatriots did, did everything he could to prevent it."

She saw there was a different expression in Patrick's eyes than there had been before and he said:

"Thank you, Rocana, and I shall certainly think over what you have said. Where am I to meet Caroline this evening?"

"In the usual place about half after seven," Rocana said, "and now I must hurry back or I shall get into trouble."

"Thank you for coming," Patrick said.

But Rocana was already galloping as quickly as she could towards the Castle.

Only as she hurried up the back stairs to her bedroom, praying the Duchess might not learn that she had been out riding or see her in her habit, did she wonder if she had made a mistake.

"Perhaps I ought to have told him to accept the inevitable," she thought to herself.

Then she thought she could hear her father's laughter and his voice saying:

"One has never lost the race until another horse has passed the winning-post!"

CHAPTER TWO

Caroline rode as quickly as she could away from the stables.

She avoided the front of the house in case some of the servants were looking out of the windows and kept in the shadows of the trees until she was on flat ground where she could gallop her horse.

The old groom who had taught her to ride was, she knew, so devoted that he would never tell her parents anything she did not wish them to know.

"Ye're ridin' late, M'Lady," he had said when she came into the stables.

"I feel I need some fresh air," Caroline replied, "but please do not tell Mama, or I know she will be cross with me."

"Oi don' tell 'Er Ladyship nothin'," the old groom replied. "'Er ain't interested in me 'orses."

That Caroline knew was a cardinal offence in his eyes, but it meant too that she would be safe.

Rocana had made her wait until her father and mother had left the house, but luckily people dined early in the country, and before they had gone dinner on Rocana's instructions had come upstairs to the School-Room.

It was much more cosy for the girls to eat there when they were alone, and it meant that they did not have to change into their evening gowns.

Caroline played about with her first course, then she said eagerly:

"Can I go now?"

31

Rocana looked towards the door where a young footman was bringing in a roast chicken.

She frowned at Caroline who realised she was being too impetuous, and when he had gone downstairs Rocana said:

"Go and change now, and I will say you have a headache and are not hungry."

She knew the servants would expect some explanation as to why Caroline was not eating her dinner. Life at the Castle was so quiet and dull that everything that happened however trivial was of interest.

The only person who knew what Caroline was doing was Nanny and as Caroline had been her baby and adored her, no secret could be kept from her.

"You'll get into trouble, that's what you'll do!" Nanny said as she helped Caroline into her habit.

"I am in trouble already, as you know," Caroline answered bitterly. "I do not wish to marry the Marquis, nor any other man I met in London."

"It's no use arguing with Her Grace, dearie," Nannie replied. "She's set her heart on you making a grand marriage."

"I know that," Caroline replied, "but I have no wish to be grand. I want to live in the country with lots of horses and dogs of my own, and be with somebody I love."

There was no need for Nannie to ask who that was, and as if she controlled her feelings because it would be a mistake to express them to Caroline, her lips were set in a tight line.

Picking up her riding-whip and gloves Caroline hurried down the side-staircase and out of the back door which led her quickly to the stables.

The rest of the staff were all having their supper, so she knew she would be unobserved.

At the same time, she felt that everything in the Castle menaced her, and once she was riding towards Patrick she wanted to be with him with an urgency that made her heart ache and the tears come into her eyes.

32

He was waiting for her in the centre of the wood where there was a clearing made by the wood-cutters.

He had tied up his own horse to a fallen tree and as soon as Caroline appeared he ran to her side to lift her down from the saddle.

As he did so he held her for a minute close against him, then taking her horse by the bridle tied it, as he had tied his own, so that it could not stray away.

Then as he turned round he saw Caroline was standing waiting for him in the centre of the clearing.

She had taken off her riding-hat and her fair hair gleamed in the last rays of the sun which was sinking over the horizon in a blaze of glory.

For moment they just stood looking at each other. Then Patrick held out his arms.

With a little cry Caroline ran towards him to hide her face in his shoulder and burst into tears.

"Do not cry, my darling," Patrick said. "Please do not cry like that."

"I cannot – bear it!" Caroline sobbed, "I cannot – leave you. What – shall I do? I know Mama and Papa – will never – listen to me!"

Her voice was almost incoherent with tears.

Patrick merely held her closer as if it was the only way he could comfort her.

His own face was white and drawn, and when they sat down on the trunk of a fallen tree Caroline thought she had never seen him look so serious or so old.

He took his arms from around her to hold one of her hands in both of his and he said very quietly:

"Are you sure, completely sure you do not wish to marry the Marquis?"

Caroline gave a cry.

"How can you ask me such a – silly question? I hate him, and he has no wish to . . marry me . . and if I have to . . accept him I think I shall – kill myself!"

She spoke almost hysterically in a way that was very unlike her and Patrick's fingers tightened on hers until he hurt her.

Then he said still very quietly:

"Listen to me, my darling, I have a suggestion to make, although I am half-afraid to say it."

Caroline raised her eyes to his enquiringly and he thought it was impossible for anybody to look so lovely.

Her eye-lashes were wet, and there were tears on her cheeks, yet she looked so exquisitely beautiful that Patrick wanted to sweep her into his arms and kiss her until there was no need for words.

Instead he asked:

"Do you love me enough to elope with me?"

For a moment Caroline was still and it was obvious she had not thought of such a thing. Then she asked:

"Elope – with – you?"

"It is something I should not ask you to do," Patrick said, "and it will cause a great scandal between our families, but I can think of no other way for us to be together."

"Do you really – mean that we could – run away and be – married before anybody can – stop us?" Caroline said hesitatingly.

"It will be a difficult thing to do, and your father is sure to try to find us and get the marriage annulled. So we would have to hide ourselves very cleverly."

"But I would be your wife?"

"You would be my wife!"

As Patrick spoke Caroline's eyes seemed to light up and there was a radiance in her face which swept away her misery and turned the tears on her cheeks into rainbows.

"Then let us elope," she said, "and at once – tonight – or tomorrow, as quickly as – possible!"

"My darling, do you really mean that?" Patrick asked.

Now he reached out and pulled her against him and as she raised her face to his he kissed her passionately and demandingly until he could feel her quiver against him and knew that her heart was beating as frantically as his.

34

Then resolutely he loosened his arms and moved a little away from her saying:

"We have to work things out very carefully."

"But I can be with you – and we can be – married?"

"That is what I pray we will be able to do," Patrick replied, "but it is going to be very difficult, and we must not make any mistakes or you will be brought back in disgrace and your mother will somehow contrive that we never see each other again."

Caroline gave a cry of fear and put out her hands to hold onto him.

"I must be with you – I must!" she said, "and you know I will – never – never love any man – except you!"

"My sweet, my darling," Patrick said.

He would have kissed her again, but he restrained himself.

"When is the Marquis arriving to stay?"

"The day after tomorrow."

Patrick frowned.

"As soon as that?"

"He is coming for the Steeple Chase."

"Of course and naturally he will win it. Nobody has better horses than his."

"Can we – leave before he – comes?"

Patrick sighed.

"That is impossible, and you will therefore, my sweet, have to be very clever and act what I know will be a very difficult part."

Caroline looked frightened as she asked:

"What must I . . do?"

"I have been thinking it out while I have been waiting for you," Patrick said. "It would be impossible for me to get a Special Licence to enable us to be married anywhere and also to collect enough money to support us while we go into hiding in less than a week or so."

"A week is too long!" Caroline exclaimed. "By that time the Marquis will have proposed to me."

"I know, but you will just have to tell your parents

35

that you will marry him," Patrick said harshly. "And when he asks you, appear to agree."

"You mean I – have to – accept his – offer?"

"Tell as few lies as possible," Patrick said, "but make the Marquis believe that you are ready to become his wife."

Caroline's hands tightened on his.

"I shall be – frightened!"

"But you will know you will never marry him because I am arranging everything so that we will be together, just as quickly as it is possible."

Caroline gave a sigh. Then she said:

"I will do – exactly what you – tell me to – do."

"I love you!" Patrick exclaimed. "And, my darling, I will move Heaven and Earth to make sure you will never regret giving up the position you would hold as the Marquis's wife for me."

"I just want to be with – you and to – love you," Caroline said simply.

He looked at her for a long moment before he said:

"There is one thing which makes me think that fate is on our side."

"What is that?"

"My father heard today that his younger brother – my uncle – is dying. He is a very rich man, but he never married, and has always said that I am his heir."

"I would marry you whether you were rich or poor," Caroline said quickly.

"I adore you for saying that," Patrick replied, "but it makes things very much easier, my sweet, if I have enough money to support you with all the comforts you have always had without relying on my father."

The way he spoke made Caroline say quickly:

"Do you think he will be – angry if we run – away?"

"I am afraid it will annoy him a great deal," Patrick replied, "not because he has anything against you, but because he likes to be on friendly terms with his neighbours. As you know, your father is very important in the County and could, if he wished, make things very uncomfortable for mine."

"Would – you mind that – very much?"

"I mind nothing except losing you, and I cannot contemplate what my life would be like without you, with all the agony of knowing that you were married to another man."

"It would be agony for me too!" Caroline said. "Oh, Patrick, help me to escape – and make sure – nobody finds us until it is – too late to do – anything about it."

"That is what I intend to do," Patrick said firmly.

As she looked up at him Caroline thought she had never seen him so resolute or in a way grown up.

Because they had known each other since they were children and met at all the parties that were given in the County, she had felt although he was actually four years older than she was that they were the same age.

Now for the first time she saw him as a man – a man who would look after and protect her and whom she would obey because he was wiser than she was.

"Tell me what to – do."

"It is going to be difficult," Patrick replied, "but I want you to go back to the Castle tonight determined to act so cleverly that nobody except Rocana will have the slightest suspicion that you are not delighted to marry the Marquis and enjoy the important place in Society which he would give you as his wife."

Caroline stiffened but she did not speak and Patrick went on:

"I shall not be able to meet you tomorrow because I shall have to go to London to obtain a Special Licence."

"Will that not be – dangerous?"

"I think they are strictly confidential, but to make sure I shall not use your title. Have you another name besides Caroline?"

"Yes, of course. I was christened 'Mary' after Lady Mary Brunt, who was said to be very beautiful."

"She could not have been more beautiful than you!" Patrick said in a deep voice. "Nobody could be!"

"That is what I want you to think."

For a moment they had both forgotten what they

37

were talking about, then Patrick went on:

"Just as soon as I have the Licence and enough money to keep us in hiding until everybody has accepted the situation we will go away."

"Do that quickly – very – very quickly," Caroline urged, "just in case something awful – happens and I – lose you!"

"You will never do that," Patrick answered, "and I am much more afraid of losing you."

He drew her close to him again and kissed her.

Only a long time later when they came back to reality did they realise that dusk had fallen and the first stars were coming out in the sky overhead.

"You must go back, my precious," Patrick said, and his voice was hoarse and a little unsteady.

"I want to stay with you."

"You will be with me by day and by night once we are married. My darling, you are quite certain you will not change your mind?"

"How could I?" Caroline asked. "I am yours – completely yours. I always have been, and I could not let – another man – touch me."

She hid her face against him as she said inarticulately.

"When I was in London – several of the – men with whom I – danced tried to – kiss me, but I knew I could never – feel for them what I – feel for you."

Patrick's arms tightened around her until it was difficult for her to breathe.

"That is what I thought would be happening," he said harshly, "and it tortured me!"

"There was no need, I was only – counting the days until I could come – home and see – you again."

"I adore you," Patrick said, "and I will spend my whole life trying to make you happy."

"I shall be happy," Caroline told him, "as I am now, but I was very – very – frightened until you said we could – run away together."

Patrick did not answer. He merely kissed her again.

Then as if he was trying to do what was the right thing he drew her to her feet, fetched her horse and after a last lingering kiss lifted her onto the saddle.

"'Tell Rocana what we have planned," he said, "but do not breathe a word of it to anybody else. You know 'walls have ears', and gossip travels on the wind."

"I will be very – very – careful," Caroline promised.

Patrick fetched his own horse and they rode side by side until they were in sight of the Castle.

Then he reached out and kissed Caroline's hand from which she had drawn her glove.

His lips were passionate and insistent on the softness of her palm until she quivered and he knew that she wanted him to kiss her lips.

Because he thought it might be dangerous for them to linger too long where they were, he smiled and said:

"Good-night, my darling, my precious! Remember only that I love you and you need no longer be afraid."

"And I love you!" Caroline whispered.

Then because she realised it was what he wanted she touched her horse with the whip and rode swiftly through the paddock to the back of the stables, entering the same way she had left them.

She was careful to creep up the back stairs where nobody saw her.

Then when she reached the School-Room landing she burst into Rocana's bedroom to find as she expected, her cousin was sitting up in bed reading.

"You are back!" Rocana exclaimed.

Caroline shut the door.

Rocana thought that she had never seen her look so happy as she reached the bed and sat down beside her.

"Oh, Rocana, everything is wonderful!"

Then in a very low voice she told Rocana what Patrick had planned they would do.

．．．．．．．

The Marquis arrived at the Castle at exactly the time he intended to do which was five o'clock in the evening.

He knew from long experience that it was always wise to arrive to stay with people so that there was less than an hour to make conversation before it was time to change for dinner.

He had planned it, as he planned everything else, down to the last minute, and as his Phaeton drawn by four superlative horses turned in at the ornamental iron gates of Bruntwick Castle, he drew a gold watch from his waist-coat pocket.

The hands pointed to three minutes to five.

His groom, who had been with him for some years and was used to his ways, remarked:

"Exactly on time, M'Lord!"

The Marquis did not reply, there was merely a faint smile on his hard lips as he looked ahead and saw Bruntwick Castle at the end of the drive.

It was an impressive sight with the Duke's standard flying from the roof, but the Marquis comparing it with his own house in Buckinghamshire thought it was somewhat of a hotch-potch contributed by various generations.

The mansion which bore his name had been completely rebuilt and redecorated by his great grandfather a hundred years ago and was a perfect example of Palladian style.

The horses although they had come from London, covered the mile-long drive in a few minutes and the Marquis drew up with a flourish outside the Castle door.

A footman had already laid a red carpet down the grey stone steps and the Butler was waiting at the top of them to greet him as he handed his reins to the groom beside him.

"As soon as you get to the stables, Jim," he said in a low voice, "see that my horses have arrived and that they are properly prepared for the Steeple Chase tomorrow."

"I'll see to it, Your Grace."

As the Phaeton moved away towards the stables the

Marquis unhurriedly and with an autocratic dignity that was characteristic of him walked up the steps and into the Hall.

He had no idea as he handed his hat to one of the footmen that high above him peeping from between the banisters Rocana was taking in every detail of his appearance.

As she looked at him she thought it was strange that he was actually so identical with the picture she had formed of him in her mind, that she might almost have created him.

He was handsome, there was no denying that, quite the most handsome man she had ever seen, but she could understand why he frightened Caroline.

Because her eyes were sharp and she was very perceptive she did not miss the hard expression in his eyes, or the fact that his mouth was so firm it might almost have been described as 'cruel'.

At the same time she appreciated his extreme elegance and the way his cravat was tied in an intricate fashion that she had never seen before.

His coat fitted without a wrinkle and his champagne-coloured pantaloons were completed by Hessian boots which reflected in their high polish the furniture past which he was walking.

As she watched him follow the Butler across the Hall towards the Red Drawing-Room where the Duke and Duchess were waiting to receive him, she was vividly conscious of his personality.

It seemed to vibrate towards her in a manner as if he came from another Planet rather than belonging to this.

Then she told herself she was being imaginative and he was just a man, if a rather extraordinary one.

Once he had disappeared into the Red Drawing-Room Rocana jumped up from where she was crouching and ran up the stairs towards the School-Room.

Caroline was waiting for her and when she appeared she asked:

"Have you seen him?"

41

"Yes, and I thought your description of him very good. He is overpowering and I am quite certain he would be overbearing with everybody, especially his wife!"

Caroline gave a little murmur of fear.

"Suppose I cannot – escape from – him?"

"You must not think like that," Rocana replied, "You must believe that everything will come right. If we want something hard enough and pray for it, our wishes always come true."

She remembered as she spoke that she had wished ever since she had come to the Castle that she could get away from it, but neither her prayers nor her wishes had been answered.

Then she told herself that at the moment she had to concentrate on Caroline and she went on in a more emphatic tone:

"Just agree to everything that is suggested, and try to look happy."

"I am frightened – very frightened!" Caroline said again. "Oh, Rocana – come downstairs – with me!"

Rocana laughed.

"Can you imagine how angry your mother would be if I did?"

"I shall make a mess of everything without – you."

"Think about Patrick, remember how much you love him and that nobody else is of any consequence."

Because Rocana spoke so firmly Caroline said meekly:

"I will – try."

She was however trembling when a footman came upstairs to say:

"Her Ladyship's wanted in the Red Drawing-Room immediately!"

Caroline went so white that Rocana was half-afraid she would faint. Then as she drew her towards the door she whispered:

"Patrick, think of Patrick as he is thinking of you."

She knew as she spoke that Patrick's name gave

Caroline courage and she walked down the stairs with her head held high.

Rocana went back into the School-Room to wait.

As she did so she saw the book she had been reading which was by Sir Walter Scott lying open and wondered if all she would know of real life would be in books.

She could feel herself thrill to the dramas that Sir Walter unfolded so brilliantly in his novels, and she lived through everything that happened to his heroines, immersing herself in them until she suffered as they suffered, she loved as they loved.

Now she went to the window to look out at the sunset thinking as she did so that her life would always be a cardboard one: made up of things rather than feelings, trivialities rather than emotions.

Because she could not help it she felt a sudden envy of Caroline that she had never felt before.

At least Caroline was living dramatically, and if she was really brave enough to elope with Patrick, she would be behaving just like the heroine of a novel, and not like the staid, rather dull daughter of a very prosaic Duke.

'She is lucky, so very lucky to have Patrick,' Rocana thought.

Then she was ashamed not just to be happy for Caroline without thinking of herself.

It seemed a long time, although it was actually not more than ten minutes, before Caroline appeared upstairs again.

She came into the room and Rocana saw at once how frightened she was.

"Is everything all right?" she asked.

It seemed difficult at first for Caroline to find her voice. Then she said:

"I think so – but, oh, Rocana, he terrified me! He seems completely menacing – just like an Ogre in a fairy-story. If he carries me away – how will Patrick ever be able to save me?"

Rocana caught hold of her hand, and it was very cold.

"Patrick is going to save you," she said, "and, Caroline, you have to act as he told you to do, as if you liked the Marquis and wish to be his wife."

"I would rather die than marry him!" Caroline exclaimed. "There is something in the way he looks at me as if I was a 'worm under his feet' which tells me that really he – despises me, and is just – making use of me for his – own ends."

"If you think that is what he is doing," Rocana said speaking calmly, "it makes it so much easier."

"Why?" Caroline enquired.

"Because if he is not in love with you he is not going to be perceptive about you. A man in love would know that you loved somebody else."

Caroline assimilated this idea for a minute. Then she said:

"You are so – sensible, Rocana. You always make me feel – brave."

"If you run away with Patrick, I will think you are the bravest person I have ever known!"

Caroline smiled.

"Will you really? I am only – brave because Patrick – loves me."

"Then that is all that matters," Rocana said. "Now come and change, Caroline, and make yourself look attractive or else the Marquis might change his mind!"

"That is what I want him to do."

Rocana shook her head.

"No, that would be a mistake. If it were not the Marquis, you know as well as I do that your mother would find somebody else equally important, and then it might not be so easy as I hope it is going to be this time, for Patrick to take you away."

As this seemed to Caroline to be logical she allowed Rocana to dress her in one of the prettiest gowns which she had brought back from London.

It was of white gauze decorated round the neck and

44

hem with small pink roses that made her look very young and spring-like.

Rocana then arranged a tiny wreath of roses at the back of her head and clasped a necklace of small pearls that her father had given her last birthday round her neck.

"You look lovely, dearest!" Rocana exclaimed.

"I wish Patrick could see me!"

"Just keep thinking that he will in a short time be seeing you every day for the rest of your lives."

"I can think of nothing else," Caroline confessed.

Then because they both knew it would be a mistake for her to be late for dinner Rocana took her to the top of the stairs and watched her walk down them, thinking how beautiful she looked.

Then as she went off into the School-Room she caught a glimpse of herself in one of the mirrors that was hung on the landing outside.

She was wearing a gown that Caroline had discarded before she went to London.

It was shabby and Caroline had been wearing it for two years before the Duchess had given it to her.

Caroline's clothes were the only things she had to wear because she had grown out of the gowns she had worn before going into mourning for her father.

But the Duchess made sure that those that were passed down to her were the least becoming of anything that Caroline owned.

She was also mean enough to remove any trimmings that might have embellished the gowns and made them more attractive.

Usually Rocana had ceased to care what she wore or how she looked, but just for a moment she envisaged herself wearing a gown like Caroline's.

She knew because she resembled her cousin, but more especially her mother, she would look very attractive.

Then with a little smile she told herself that only in

her dreams would she wear such gowns, and it was no use thinking about it.

. . . .

Once again Rocana was in bed and reading the last chapter of "Ivanhoe" when Caroline came into her bedroom.

She put down her book and sat up a little further against the pillows as her cousin shut the door and came across to the bed to say in a voice that was little louder than a whisper:

"He has asked me to – marry him and says he – wishes the wedding to take place in – ten days time!"

Rocana stared at her cousin incredulously.

"I cannot believe it!"

"That is what he said, and he made an excuse for such haste that he has to go to Paris on business which concerns the Prince Regent, and he thought how – pleasant it would be for us to spend our – honeymoon – there!"

Caroline spoke as if the words were wrenched from her lips and Rocana said:

"Surely Aunt Sophie did not agree?"

"He had already talked to Papa and Mama and they not only agreed, but thought it was a delightful idea for me to go to Paris."

Rocana did not speak and Caroline went on:

"They were quite agreeable for the wedding to be small and take place here with only our friends and relations and just a few of the Marquis's who are prepared to make the journey from London."

"He must be in more of a mess than we imagined!" Rocana said reflectively.

"I must tell Patrick at once!" Caroline exclaimed.

"You will see him tomorrow at the Steeple Chase," Rocana replied. "I was going to advise you not to speak to him in front of anybody else, but I dare say you will be able to pretend to be making a fuss of his horse."

She paused then added urgently:

"But do be careful! If anybody sees you looking at each other they would guess that you are in love!"

"We must run away at the weekend," Caroline said, "or the very latest the beginning of next week!"

"Of course," Rocana agreed.

Then as she spoke the door opened and both she and Caroline gasped as the Duchess came into the room.

For one terrified moment Rocana thought she must have heard what her daughter just said.

But surprisingly her Aunt was smiling and she said in a quite pleasant tone to Caroline:

"I thought I would find you here, telling Rocana the good news!"

Nervously Caroline got to her feet.

"Yes, Mama – that is what I was – telling her."

"You are a very lucky girl! And although it seems extraordinary that you should be married in such a hurry, I do understand the dear Marquis's wishes to take you to Paris with him."

"Yes, Mama."

"Of course," the Duchess went on, "it leaves very little time for you and me to buy your trousseau."

"My – trousseau?" Caroline repeated rather stupidly.

"You can hardly be married without one," the Duchess said, "and considering the position your Bridegroom holds, what you wear will be of extreme importance!"

She gave an exasperated sigh before she went on:

"I had been planning that you would outshine every bride there has ever been, and certainly your wedding-gown must be sensational. But while we will get as many gowns as possible ready before the happy day, the rest can be finished by the time you return to England."

Caroline did not speak, she could only look at her mother with the expression of a frightened rabbit.

Rocana held her breath as she knew already what the Duchess was going to say next.

"You and I will leave tomorrow morning as early as possible for London," the Duchess continued. 'You will miss the Steeple Chase but that will not matter, for the Marquis has already said that he is returning to London when it is over and will not be staying to dinner."

"We are – going to – London, Mama?"

"Do not be stupid, Caroline," the Duchess said sharply. "We can hardly choose your clothes while we are sitting here at the Castle!"

She turned to look at Rocana and went on:

"You had better get up, Rocana, and start packing for Caroline. It is too late to wake Nanny, but she and the Housemaids can finish off anything you have forgotten in the morning."

"Yes, Aunt Sophie."

"And try not to forget anything," the Duchess continued her voice sharpening. "You know how careless you can be when you waste your brain poring over books, instead of attending to more practical matters."

She looked disparagingly at 'Ivanhoe' and moving towards the door she said:

"Your father and I are very happy, Caroline, that you will be the wife of a very important man, and when we are in London I shall take the opportunity of instructing you as to what will be required of you when you take your position at his side at Court ceremonies."

With an unmistakable look of satisfaction in her eyes the Duchess walked out of the room closing the door behind her.

Neither of the girls spoke until they could no longer hear her heavy footsteps going down the stairs.

Then Caroline gave a cry like a small animal that has been caught in a trap.

"If I am to be in London – with Mama," she cried, "how can I – run away with – Patrick?"

She sounded so desperate that Rocana said quickly:

"You will have to come back here for the wedding, and I am sure he will think of some way to get you away in time."

48

"Supposing Mama keeps me there until the last moment? You know what she is like when she is worrying over clothes!"

"You will have to come back eventually," Rocana persisted.

"Patrick meant to leave – before that."

"I will see Patrick," Rocana promised, "and although it will be difficult, I will somehow get a message to you. I will write in a very guarded way and you will have to read between the lines."

She thought before she added:

"It will be a kind of code."

"Suppose I do not understand and Mama reads it?"

"We will give Patrick the name of one of the horses or something like that," Rocana answered. "Leave it to me. I will think of something before tomorrow morning."

"But I cannot go to London!" Caroline cried. "Perhaps I can be ill so that it will be impossible for Mama to take me."

"You have to go," Rocana replied. "There is no other way. But you must write and tell me on what day you are coming back, and I will tell Patrick so that he can make his plans accordingly."

She saw that Caroline was trembling and on the verge of tears, so she got out of bed and sitting beside her, she put her arms around her.

"You have to be brave," she said. "These are only obstacles to be overcome before you can be with Patrick and free of the Marquis."

"Supposing they are – too high and I cannot – escape before I am – married to him?"

"You will escape," Rocana said firmly. " 'I feel it in my bones,' as Nanny would say."

Then as she felt Caroline was not convinced she said:

"I feel it in another way too, which Papa always used to say was part of the magic Mama had."

"Do you mean – clairvoyantly?" Caroline asked with a sob in her voice.

"Rather like that," Rocana agreed, "but it is more a kind of instinct, or a feeling inside me, that tells me when things will come right, however difficult they may appear."

She thought as she spoke of how in the past she had known beforehand not only when things had come right, but when they were going to be wrong.

When her mother had been bitten by a snake when they were walking through long grass one very hot summer she had known that she would die, even though the doctors were quite certain the bite was not really serious.

She had known, although she would not face it even to herself, when her father had gone out hunting on a cold winter's day when there was frost in the air and he had expected to be home early, that he would not return.

She had gone out to the stables and said:

"It is a rotten day for hunting. Do not go, Papa! Please, stay here!"

"Whether it is rotten or not," her father had replied, "I need the exercise. Besides, dearest, there are some friends I promised to see. If I am late, you will know that I have stopped to have a drink with them."

He had kissed her and swung himself into the saddle before looking down and adding:

"I wish you were coming with me, but we will ride together tomorrow. Take care of yourself."

It was what she wanted to say to him as he had ridden away.

She had watched him go, and in some strange way she could not account for to herself she had known that he was riding with his top-hat at a raffish angle out of her life and they would not be together tomorrow morning.

Now she said to Caroline and there was a note in her voice that was very convincing:

"I promise you, dearest, however difficult it will be, however many fences we have to jump on the way, you will reach the winning-post and marry Patrick."

"You are sure – really sure? Can you see with your 'Magic Eye' that it will – come true?"

"My 'Magic Eye' never lies," Rocana smiled. "You will never be the Marchioness of Quorn, but the wife of Patrick Fairley."

Caroline threw her arms around her neck and kissed her cheek.

"That is what I want more than anything in all the world and I believe you, Rocana – I do really – believe you!"

CHAPTER THREE

Rocana waited until she had seen Caroline, the
Duchess and Nanny off immediately breakfast was
over and then hurried upstairs to change into her
riding-habit.

As she did so she knew she was neglecting the Duchess's last instructions which had been very explicit.

She had called Rocana in her room as she and Caroline were going downstairs and pointing to a large
pile of garments on a chair she said:

"While I am away you will mend these, and I shall be
extremely annoyed if they are not finished by the time I
return."

She spoke in that sharp, harsh voice which
expressed her dislike of her niece and which was
echoed by the expression in her eyes.

Rocana did not speak and after a moment the
Duchess went on:

"I have been thinking over what you will do when
Caroline is married. I have now decided that you will
concentrate on your sewing."

Rocana stiffened and the Duchess said:

"I have no intention of allowing you to waste your
time as you do at the moment riding and reading. You
will work in the capacity of sewing-maid and I shall
make sure that you spend your time more usefully than
you have been doing up until now."

She paused and her eyes rested on Rocana's face as
she said:

"After all, you must expect to make some contribution towards the money your Uncle has had to expend on paying your father's debts, and also make some reparation for the fact that your mother's kith and kin were killing and crippling our soldiers and sailors for over fifteen years."

Rocana clenched her hands together in the effort to control the protest that rose to her lips.

None of her mother's family had served in the Napoleonic Army.

Her grandfather had always, her mother told her, deprecated the war and had despised the jumped-up aristocracy that the victorious Corsican created in place of the *ancien regime* to which all the old aristocratic families in France belonged.

But she knew it was hopeless to say this to the Duchess who had hated her mother and her father as she hated her.

She therefore kept silent, and as if the Duchess was somewhat piqued at getting no response she said:

"Mind these things are repaired and done properly or I shall certainly punish you severely for your negligence!"

With that she flounced out of the room and down the stairs to join Caroline who was waiting in the Hall.

As Rocana followed her Aunt she knew by the expression on Caroline's face that she was apprehensive as to what her mother had said to her.

She was suffering so acutely at leaving Patrick that it was hard to pretend to be looking forward to the journey to London.

As she kissed Rocana goodbye she whispered so that nobody else could hear:

"Write as – soon as you – see him. I must know what he – thinks."

Rocana thought it was dangerous to say anything so she merely nodded her head, and Caroline with a woebegone expression waved her hand as the carriage drove away down the drive.

. . . .

The Duke and the Marquis had already left to greet the first arrivals from the Steeple Chase.

However much she might be punished for negligence, Rocana had no intention of missing the race.

She therefore hurried into her habit and running down the back stairs reached the stables after most of the grooms had left for the starting point, which was at the north end of the Park where the trees ended and the flat ground began.

Rocana was aware there would be a large crowd of spectators and she therefore was careful to avoid being seen as she moved through the orchard: riding to the south of the area, marked out for the race.

There was a place where she could watch the start and almost the whole of the rest of the course as well.

The last jump was just below her, and the winning-post a quarter-of-a-mile ahead.

She was sheltered from being seen by trees, and as she drew her horse to a stand-still she wished that Caroline could be with her so that they could laugh together at some of the entries and admire the others.

There were a number of horses milling about round the start and Rocana could see the Duke was trying to create some order.

She was certain he was being irritated by the spectators who got in the way and their dogs who barked at the horses causing them to rear and buck.

Then as she watched, she saw the Marquis join the Duke and thought that nobody could fail to recognise him, and that Patrick had been right when he said he would undoubtedly be the winner.

He was riding a large black stallion and Rocana knew it would be difficult for any of the other contestants to rival such a magnificent animal.

At the same time Patrick was on a well-bred horse he had broken in himself, and he had the advantage of being familiar with the course which was laid out in the shape of a large horse-shoe.

He had been over the jumps a dozen times in the last

week or so, as had some of the other contestants who lived in the vicinity of the Castle.

There were one or two quite comic entrants, mostly yeoman farmers who knew they had no chance of winning, even if they could finish the course, but who just wanted to join in the fun.

Because Rocana had good eye-sight she could see them all very clearly from where she had stationed herself on top of a small hill, and she was surprised that nobody else had chosen this particular vantage point.

Instead there were spectators at every jump and she knew that the rest of the crowd would watch the start, then immediately run as quickly as they could to the finishing-point.

The horses had been got into some semblance of a line and she saw the Duke waiting for one awkward animal who would not turn in the right direction. Then he dropped the flag he was carrying.

There were off!

Rocana held her breath as she saw a big field thunder down to the first fence.

She had jumped it herself and knew that unless one took it at exactly the right angle it was tricky.

She was therefore not surprised to see two horses fall. One of them got up and galloped after the others, determined not to be out of the race.

A riderless horse was always a danger and was responsible for another fall at the next fence, a second riderless horse joining the others.

The next three were fairly easy and there were no casualties, and with a sigh of relief Rocana saw that one of the riderless horses had run out and been caught by a groom.

Then came some really hard riding over heavy ground that was always damp whatever the time of year, but she could see the Marquis was taking it in his stride.

Although he was riding his stallion with a tight rein,

he was slightly ahead of the rest of the field.

After four more fences some of the farmers dropped out finding the going too rough, two horses refused to jump, and one threw his rider over his head.

Now they had almost completed the first round of the course and swinging to the left to avoid the winning-post were back at the first fence to start all over again.

The riders had now thinned out considerably and the Marquis was a length ahead, his horse jumping each fence with a foot to spare, and treating the easier ones with a disdain which Rocana could sense even from such a long distance away.

She was aware too that the Marquis rode better than anybody she had ever seen with the exception of her father.

Or perhaps to be honest she should say he was as good as her father had been and seemed to be part of his horse and the mere fact of riding such a fine animal seemed to give him a sense of omnipotence.

She had the feeling, although she could not hear him, that when he took a difficult fence he encouraged his horse by speaking to it as her father had always taught her to do.

Once she saw him bend forward, pat his horse on the neck after he had negotiated a difficult fence, avoided a riderless horse, and ignored a spectator who was in the way.

Then, two fences from the end, the Marquis was challenged.

To her delight Rocana saw that it was Patrick!

He had been riding a little way back and she thought on a tight rein.

Now he gave his horse his head and as he took the last fence but one at exactly the same time as the Marquis he bent forward and was obviously ready to ride all out for the rest of the race.

Rocana could not be sure, but she felt the Marquis was surprised.

Quite suddenly the race that had seemed a walk-over for him became a contest.

Now the two men were really struggling – although the Marquis was not aware they were also rivals in another field – and riding all out, each one determined to be the winner.

They took the last fence with not an inch to choose between them, and then there was a clear run to the winning-post.

Most of the spectators had reached it by this time and Rocana could hear their cheers of encouragement echo over the whole valley.

The two horses were galloping at a phenomenal speed, the turf from their hoofs flying out behind them, and she knew that each man was straining every nerve to beat the other.

Then with a roar of voices which echoed and re-echoed they were neck and neck as they passed the Duke who was waiting for them.

From where Rocana was watching it was impossible to be sure which of them was the winner.

She could only hope it was Patrick, because it would be a good omen for him and Caroline.

Then she knew that now the race was over she must not linger, but must get back to the Castle and think of some way by which she could communicate with Patrick before he went home.

It was a relief to think as she rode back that she need not be afraid of being seen by the Duchess who had already told her that she was not to attend the Steeple Chase and was on no account to be seen by anybody who had been invited to the Castle for luncheon.

It was so usual for her to be isolated in obscurity that Rocana had hardly listened at the time.

It was only this morning when she awoke to finish Caroline's packing that she had realised with a lilt in her heart she would be able to see the race without there being a row about it afterwards.

She rode into the stables knowing she would be back before the grooms and put her own horse into his stall, took off his bridle and unsaddled him.

She was just about to leave when she heard a commotion at the other end of the stable.

There were twenty stalls in this particular building and she was aware there was a horse plunging about and several grooms shouting at each other.

Because she was curious she walked down the alleyway between the stalls noting which of the Duke's horses were still in them.

She found, as she expected, that the commotion was coming from one of the stalls where visiting guests usually stabled their horses.

When she reached it she saw an extremely finelooking animal almost, she thought, the counterpart of the one the Marquis had been riding in the race.

He was rearing up on his hind legs and making it impossible for the grooms to put his bridle over his head.

In fact it was quite obvious that the three grooms watching him were nervous, and the one who was holding the bridle in his hand appeared to be whitefaced and shaking.

"What is the matter?" Rocana asked in her soft voice.

The three men looked at her and she saw they were all strangers.

"It's this 'ere stallion 'Is Lordship bought last week, Miss," the oldest of the grooms replied.

"He seems rather wild," Rocana observed with a smile.

"There's no 'oldin' 'im, Miss, and that's the truth!" the groom replied. " 'Is Lordship made us bring 'im 'ere in case he decided to ride 'im instead of 'Conqueror' an' I don't know 'ow we're goin' to get 'im back 'ome again."

"Is His Lordship thinking of riding him?" Rocana asked.

"No, Miss, this'n 'Vulcan's 'is name, and the one he's bin ridin' 'ave to be ridden by the out-riders. Jed's supposed to ride this'n."

"Oi ain't ridin' 'im!" Jed remarked quickly. " 'E'd kill me, an' Oi don't want to die yet!"

"Surely His Lordship does not want you to saddle him before luncheon?" Rocana asked.

" 'Is Lordship's orders, Miss," the groom who had been speaking to her before said, "is that he'll leave as soon as possible after the race an' we daren't keep 'im waitin'!"

The other grooms nodded agreement of this and one said:

"We all be's 'fraid of the Master's anger."

"Oi ain't ridin' 'im, I tells yer, I ain't ridin' 'im!" Jed cried frantically.

"Nobody ain't gonna ride 'im if'n we don't get this bridle on 'im," the other groom replied.

"Let me try," Rocana said.

There was a look of surprise on their faces and for a moment they did not seem to grasp what she meant.

Then as she opened the door of the stall the oldest groom said quickly:

"Nay, Miss, ye can't go in wi' *Vulcan*! When 'e's like this 'e'll kill ye fer sure!"

"I do not think so," Rocana answered quietly. "Keep still, and do not talk."

She walked into the stall, speaking very softly as she did so in the voice she had heard her father use when he was breaking in one of his wild horses.

He bought them cheap and invariably turned them into perfectly-trained animals which he either rode himself or sold at a handsome profit.

"Why are you upset?" she was saying softly. "I expect it is because they did not allow you to take part in the race, which was very unfair. You are so beautiful, so magnificent, I am sure you would have won it easily. There will be other races, you may be sure of that. But you want them to admire you and feel happy when they are riding on your back."

She went on talking standing by the side of the stall, making no effort to approach *Vulcan* who was watching her warily, his ears twitching as he appeared to listen to what she was saying.

Still talking, still praising and admiring him in her father's voice which she had always thought to herself had a mesmeric magic about it and was somehow irresistible, she moved slowly towards him.

Some of the tension seemed to go out of *Vulcan* and he made no effort to rear.

Rocana moved nearer and nearer to him until she was touching him, patting first his neck, then caressing his nose and his ears until, as if he enjoyed it, when she stopped he nuzzled against her.

It was only then, not raising her voice but using the same tone with which she had spoken to *Vulcan* she said:

"Give me the bridle!"

Nervously the groom who was holding it came into the stall and held it out to her at arm's length.

She took it in her right hand, still soothing *Vulcan* gently with her left. Then as she slipped the bridle over his head she said to him:

"You do not want to stay in here on such a lovely day. I will take you outside in the sunshine. You will find it is much more enjoyable than trying to dance about in a place that is much too small for a big, powerful horse like you!"

The bridle was over *Vulcan's* head and now she turned him round and led him from the stall and as she did so she saw where there had been three men watching her there were now four.

For a moment she looked into the Marquis's eyes and knew the expression on his face was of astonishment.

Then deliberately ignoring him she led *Vulcan* out of the stall past her small audience and into the stable-yard.

She was still talking to him, telling him how much he would enjoy himself outside and that everybody would admire him.

Then she drew him to a stand-still and said in the same voice as she had used before:

"Put his saddle on, and very gently."

She felt *Vulcan* stiffen as somebody came up beside him and as Rocana held the bridle tightly to prevent him from rearing, she realised incredulously that it was the Marquis.

He put the saddle on the horse's back gently in exactly the way she wished it to be done.

Then as a groom hastily fastened the girths on either side the Marquis stood beside her to ask:

"Who are you? And how can you know how to handle a horse like this in such an amazing manner?"

Rocana looked up at him and smiled.

When she had gone into *Vulcan's* stall she had automatically pulled off her riding-hat from her head because she thought it might get in the way.

Now with the sunshine on her hair she looked very small and insubstantial beside the huge stallion.

The Marquis too was so tall that she had to tip back her head to look up at him, and as he looked down at her she saw the surprise in his eyes.

"*Vulcan* was only showing off, and horses always know when people are afraid of them," she replied. "It makes them behave defiantly."

"What is your name?" the Marquis asked.

"Rocana."

She had not meant to say any more but she realised he was waiting and after a moment she added a little reluctantly.

". . . Brunt!"

"A member of the Duke's family! I did not meet you last night, or perhaps you have only just arrived."

"No, I live here."

As soon as she spoke she realised she should not be talking to the Marquis and if the Duchess learned of it she would be furious. She said quickly:

"*Vulcan* will be all right now, but I think perhaps you should ride him yourself and teach him how to behave."

"Are you giving me instructions?" the Marquis asked somewhat mockingly.

61

"No, no! I was merely making a suggestion, and let me congratulate you on a very exciting finish to the Steeple Chase."

Then, as if she could not help asking the question, she added:

"Who did win?"

"We agreed it was a dead heat," the Marquis replied and knew by the expression on Rocana's face that she was pleased.

She put the reins she was holding into the Marquis's hand and said:

"It was very exciting. And I think your horses are magnificent!"

She turned away before he could answer and ran across the yard remembering as she did so, that she had left her hat in the stable.

Only when she reached her bedroom did she think how exciting it had been to manage *Vulcan* in the way she had, and also to meet the Marquis.

But she could understand how much he frightened Caroline and also apparently those who served him.

"He really is overwhelming!" she told herself.

It was almost like confronting a typhoon or a tidal wave or, she thought with a little smile, taking a fence that was so high it seemed impossible to leap over it.

'I should not have met him now,' she thought, 'and I may never meet him again, but I shall find it difficult to forget him.'

Leaning out of the window she could see a number of the riders entering the Castle for luncheon that had been prepared for them in the big Baronial Hall.

She was aware that the Cooks had been working all the week for the feast, for it was nothing else, that everybody expected at the Castle.

There would be, Rocana knew, great haunches of venison from the deer in the Park, boars's heads and suckling pigs, besides innumerable legs of lamb, chickens, fat pigeons, and trout from the lake.

This was always an all-male party as some of the

competitors were not considered well-bred enough to mix with the Duchess and certainly not with Caroline.

Therefore even if the Duchess had not gone to London, she would not have seen the Marquis at luncheon although he might have expected to say goodbye to her before he left.

Rocana had a sudden impulse to take Caroline's place and somehow contrive to be in the Drawing-Room where the Marquis would say goodbye to her Uncle.

She had a feeling she would like to talk to him again and to assess in her own mind exactly what he was like.

It had been difficult to think of him clearly when she had been concentrating on *Vulcan*.

At the same time she thought it was interesting to meet a man with such a strong personality that he would dominate any company in which he found himself.

He also, she remembered, had a reputation which ensured that he was talked about from one end of the country to the other.

"I think he is hard, and he could be cruel if it suited him," Rocana ruminated, "not to animals, but to people."

She was thinking of the women who supposedly had committed suicide for love of him, or died of a broken heart, but she felt they must have been weak, ineffective creatures.

At the same time, it was obvious that a strong personality always attracted those who were weaker and wished to cling to him 'like barnacles on the bottom of a boat', as her father had once said.

"How can you be so rude about us poor women?" her mother asked.

"As a woman you should understand," her father replied. "Those who cling like creeping ivy to a man stifle him to the point where he either accepts being imprisoned by them, or fights himself free."

"I think you are just making excuses for your own sex when they are ruthless, and certainly heartless," her mother protested.

Rocana had known she was arguing with her father because they both enjoyed it, and she was aware that her mother always stimulated her father's mind.

They therefore had arguments which made it seem to her as if sparks flew like shimmering fireflies backwards and forwards across the table.

After a minute her mother would laugh and say:

"You win! You are too clever for me, darling, and I admit that I am only a weak little woman while you are a superior, dominating man!"

"One who lies adoring at your feet," her father had replied once. "You know as well as I do that you twist me round your little finger, and always and inevitably you get your own way!"

Her mother had wanted to argue but he kissed her and said to Rocana:

"I hope you are listening, my little one, and making notes of how a clever woman can out-wit any man, whether he is a King or a crossing sweeper."

"You know that is untrue," her mother protested, "and Rocana has to learn that women always must take second place and be the shadow of the throne! At the same time, it is easier to get your own way with love."

Rocana thought this was true, but in the case of the Marquis he obviously had too much of it and as he acquired it too easily he would inevitably find it boring and throw it away.

Then she told herself love was not like that, not the love that existed between her father and her mother, and which she was sure was the love that Caroline and Patrick had for each other.

That sort of love did not grow stale or wither, but increased, deepened and became more wonderful year by year.

'Perhaps that is what the Marquis has never found,' she thought.

Then she told herself that what really mattered was to prevent him from making Caroline unhappy as he had made so many other women.

Her instinct told her that he would always frighten Caroline and her sweetness would not interest him for long.

She had the idea that what he really needed in a woman was a challenge, just as a horse like *Vulcan* presented a challenge because he had to dominate him.

At the same time he would only gain complete mastery over such a horse by using the same magic she had used to make him docile and obedient.

"I am wasting my time thinking of him," she admonished herself. "Once he is Caroline's husband, it is unlikely that I shall ever see him again, and if he is bored and unhappy it would be his own fault for being so overpowering."

What she had to do now was to find Patrick and tell him what had happened to Caroline.

She crept down the stairs, afraid of being seen, and managed while the servants were busy in the Dining-Room to climb quietly up the small stairway which led into the Minstrels' Gallery.

The Minstrels' Gallery was disguised by a screen of thick wood carving so that while the minstrels could peep through it onto the guests below, those looking up from the Dining-Room table could hear the music, but not see who played it.

Now as Rocana opened the door there was the sound of laughter from those in the Hall below which struck her like a strong wind.

She moved quietly to the screen and looking down saw first the Duke sitting at the end of the table in a high-backed chair surmounted by a Ducal crown.

The Marquis was on his right and Patrick on the opposite side of the table a few places down.

All the guests were enjoying themselves uproariously, toasting each other across the table and piling their plates with everything that was being offered to them on huge crested silver dishes.

Rocana noticed that the Marquis had very little on his plate and had hardly touched the wine in his glass.

The Duke however, as if he had found the morning strenuous, although he had not taken part in the race, was drinking more Claret than usual.

The Butler was filling his glass, and he seemed in a good humour.

He was talking quite animatedly to the Marquis, and although Rocana could not hear what was being said she had the feeling he was discussing the wedding and revealing how gratified he was to have the Marquis as his son-in-law.

It was just an impression she had almost as if she could read the thoughts of those she was watching.

Then as she looked across the table to where Patrick was sitting she was certain that her supposition was right.

Patrick was scowling and he had pushed his plate away as if he was not hungry.

She stood watching and long before the luncheon was finished the Marquis rose and she knew that he was saying he must leave.

The Duke rose too and Rocana thought he was expostulating and telling him not to be in any hurry.

They walked towards the door side by side and the guests at the table lifted their glasses as the Marquis toasted him:

"Jolly good show, My Lord!" "All the best for the rest of the Season!" "You'll be the winner at Doncaster!"

"Thank you," the Marquis replied, "but I never count my horses before they cross the line!"

There was a roar of laughter at this and they were still drinking his health as he and the Duke left the room.

As they disappeared, Rocana saw Patrick rise too and knew he wanted to get away because he was worried about Caroline.

She thought it unlikely that anybody would have told him that she had already left for London.

He would therefore be wondering why he had not seen her, and hoping she would be waiting for him in the wood which was on his way home.

Not hurrying, because she wished him to leave the stable first as it would be a mistake for them to meet there, Rocana found her way to the stall in which she had put her horse before luncheon.

As she passed the end of the stable-yard she saw the Marquis had taken longer to leave than she expected, and was only now driving away from the front door.

She stood in the shadows of the shrubs and watched him go, knowing that his Phaeton which was built for speed was the smartest and most up-to-date model she had ever seen and that the four horses he was driving were superlative.

The Marquis himself seemed part of the whole *entourage* and made Rocana feel he had stepped out of a novel, and was not real.

Then as she saw *Vulcan* being ridden by one of the out-riders in his black velvet cap and white wig she thought with a smile that he was behaving better than anybody could have hoped.

She was however sure that the Marquis had his eye on him in case there was any trouble.

Then as the small cavalcade passed over the bridge and started along the mile-long drive bordered by oak-trees, she knew that now the Marquis was out of the way she must concentrate on Patrick.

She saddled her own horse as she had done so often at home and rode out of the stables before any of the Duke's grooms had any idea she had been there.

She rode the route that she and Caroline always used when they did not wish to be seen, and when she reached the centre of the wood she found as she had hoped that Patrick was there.

He had tied up his horse and as soon as she appeared

hurried to her side to lift her down from the saddle saying as he did so:

"Where is Caroline? What has happened? I thought she would be at the race?"

Rocana waited until he had attached the bridle of her horse to a fallen tree, then she said:

"The Duchess has already taken Caroline to London to buy her trousseau!"

Patrick looked worried.

"I never thought of that."

"Nor did we until last night," Rocana replied, "and it was very stupid of us. Of course Aunt Sophie is determined that as Caroline is making such a brilliant marriage she must have a trousseau fit for a Queen!"

Patrick did not smile. Instead he said:

"I was desperately afraid I would not see you or Caroline because my Uncle has died."

"Does that mean you have to go away?" Rocana asked.

"Yes, for at least three or four days."

"As Caroline will also be away for as long as that, or perhaps more, I will write and tell her not to worry about you."

"Was she worrying about me?"

"She was so miserable that she could not say 'goodbye'."

"You will be writing to her?"

"Yes, very guardedly in a kind of code, just in case Aunt Sophie sees my letter."

"Then tell her, if you can, that I think my Uncle's death will help us because I shall now have all the money I need."

Patrick paused. Then he asked in a very different voice:

"When will Caroline be back?"

Rocana made a little helpless gesture with her hands.

"I have no idea, but she has promised to let me know exactly what has been planned. When shall I meet you here again? Next Monday?"

"I thought myself I would be back on Sunday night, or

Monday morning,'' Patrick said. "The Funeral should be over by then.''

"I hope I shall have some news for you.''

"Thank you, Rocana,'' he said. "Did you watch the race?''

She smiled before she added:

"I thought it was a good omen for you and Caroline that you rode so magnificently, and it was a dead heat.''

"I wanted to beat him!'' Patrick said fiercely.

"I can understand that, but because he had such an outstanding horse, and is undoubtedly the finest rider one could imagine, it was fantastic the way you challenged him.''

"I would still like to have beaten him,'' Patrick said, "and it is what I intend to do where Caroline is concerned!''

He spoke with a determination which Rocana thought he had never had before, and she said:

"That is a race you will win! And I have convinced Caroline that my 'Magic Eye' tells me you will both be very happily married.''

Patrick smiled for the first time since she had joined him.

"Thank you, Rocana,'' he said, "and after we are married I promise you that Caroline and I will do something about you.''

"About me?'' Rocana repeated in surprise.

"You do not suppose everybody is not aware of the disgraceful way you are treated by your Aunt and Uncle?''

"Everybody?''

"Everybody who knew your father loved him, and it is a shame and a scandal that you never go anywhere and are treated as if you were a nobody, instead of taking your rightful place as your father's daughter.''

Because what Patrick said was so unexpected Rocana felt the tears come into her eyes.

"Thank you for .. saying that,'' she managed to say after a moment, "not only .. because you are so kind to me .. but because you have .. reassured me that ..

Papa is not . . forgotten."

"Of course no one has forgotten him!" Patrick retorted. "Everyone loved your father, and those who knew her loved your mother."

He sighed.

"If only Lord Leo had been the Duke I should not have to make Caroline run away with me, and cause a scandal."

"Does the idea upset you?" Rocana enquired.

Patrick smiled again.

"Not really," he said. "All I want is Caroline's happiness, and I know that she would never be happy with the Marquis, nor with any other man for that matter."

"Just as I said to Caroline," Rocana answered, "your difficulties are just hurdles or fences, which you have to jump before you reach the winning-post."

"You are right," Patrick agreed, "and come hell or high water, Caroline is going to be mine, and I will kill anyone who tried to prevent me!"

He spoke so violently that Rocana looked up at him in surprise.

Then she told herself that love had changed him into a man who knew his own mind and was determined whatever the cost to get what he wanted.

"I must go back," she said, "because it would be a great mistake for anybody to know that we are plotting together. But I will be here on Monday and I hope with good news."

"By that time," Patrick said in a low voice, "I shall have the Special Licence, and I hope a fortune with which I can give Caroline everything she wants."

"I think all she really wants is you," Rocana replied, and saw that what she said brought a light to his eyes.

He lifted her into the saddle and watched her ride away back to the Castle before he mounted and rode off in the opposite direction.

Only as she saw the Castle ahead of her did Rocana remember the amount of sewing which the Duchess had left for her to do.

It meant that to make up for her having wasted most of the day she would have to sit up half the night besides spending almost every moment stitching away until the Duchess returned.

"I doubt if she will be back before the end of the week!" she consoled herself.

The ten days in which the Marquis had said he must be married would end on Sunday.

It seemed a strange day of the week for a Society wedding, but the Marquis was a law unto himself, and if he wished to be married on a Sunday, on a Sunday it would be.

'It is therefore certain,' Rocana thought as she reached the stables, 'that Caroline will return by Thursday, at the very latest.'

It did not give them a lot of time, but the Duchess would be determined to make the future Marchioness of Quorn a 'fashion-plate' for other ambitious brides to admire, and of course envy.

CHAPTER FOUR

Riding towards the wood Rocana was wondering what she could say to Patrick because everything they had planned was falling to pieces around their ears.

She had been astonished when late last night a Post Chaise had arrived from London bringing her a letter from Caroline.

When she opened it she realised that it was not only urgent, but so secret that Caroline had done the only sensible thing she could which was to get Nanny to send it by Post Chaise and not trust the Mail.

The letter was written obviously in haste and anguish because Caroline's usually elegant writing was little more than a scrawl.

Rocana read:

"Dearest Rocana,

I am sending this to You by Post Chaise because Patrick must know at Once what has Happened. I am absolutely Desperate, and there is Nothing I can do but Pray that somehow, despite Everything he will Rescue me.

Mama and the Marquis had quite a disagreeable Argument this morning when He came to the House just as we were going shopping to say that He had to be in Paris by Tuesday and He suggested We should Change the Wedding day to Saturday.

I foolishly, had been quite Certain we were Leaving on Thursday at the Latest, but Mama told the Marquis we should not be back at the Castle until

Saturday afternoon at about Five o'clock.

He said it was Ridiculous that Everything should be dependent on the Delivery of a Wedding gown, but you know what Mama is like when She has made up her Mind, and finally He capitulated, but very Disagreeably.

Instead He said we must be Married at nine-thirty on Sunday morning, and there could be no proper Reception, but as Soon as I had Changed into my Going-away Clothes, he intended to leave Immediately for Dover.

I think it was because Mama was Frightened he might Call the Wedding off altogether that She agreed to This, but with a very bad Grace, and was so Cross to me afterwards that I burst into Tears.

Really I was Crying because I was Frightened that if we did not Arrive at the Castle until so late Patrick and I could not Elope.

Please, Rocana, see him Immediately and beg Him not to Give In, but to Take me away. The more I see of the Marquis the more He frightens Me, and I know that I cannot Live without Patrick and I would never be Happy with Anybody Else.

Nanny is going to send This to You as soon as Mama and I have left for the Shops. I am sick of Gowns and as I do not Expect ever to Wear any of Them, it is just Hours of boredom standing while the Seamstresses stick Pins into me!

Please, please, Rocana, help me! I am so Frightened and Unhappy.

With Love from
Caroline.

P.S. Please give Patrick my Clothes so that I will have Something to Wear.

P.P.S. I have put a Note in this Letter for Him."

There was a piece of paper in the envelope marked: "PATRICK" and Rocana could only hope it would cheer him up which he would obviously need after he had read Caroline's letter.

As she saw the wood in front of her she thought that perhaps a lot of the trouble was her fault.

She ought to have made Caroline realise from the beginning that she would have to marry the Marquis and say goodbye to Patrick.

But something defiant in herself made her ask why any woman should be pushed about as though she was just an inanimate object without any feelings.

It annoyed her and she would do everything in her power to help Caroline to be with the man she loved.

Patrick was waiting in the clearing as he had every day since Monday just in case either of them had any news.

Now, before she could speak he knew by the expression on her face that she had heard from Caroline.

"What does she say?" he asked eagerly.

She handed him the envelope which contained Caroline's letter to her and the note for him.

"I am afraid it is bad news," she said in a low voice.

Patrick was not listening.

He had sat down on the fallen trunk of a tree and was reading Caroline's letter, and was therefore oblivious to everything else.

Rocana sat beside him trying to think out some sensible plan, but knowing it was going to be very difficult.

Even if he and Caroline eloped as soon as she arrived they would not be very far away by the time her absence was discovered.

This meant that the Duke might be able to catch up with them before they were married.

He had a large number of grooms and very fast horses, and Rocana knew there were only a certain number of main roads in the County on which Caroline and Patrick could travel to wherever they intended to hide.

She was calculating how many hours they would have before the Duke and Duchess would be aware that she was not in the Castle when Patrick looked up and said:

74

"This is what I was expecting."

"You were?"

"I was quite certain that the Duchess with her grandiose ideas of what the Marquis's bride should look like would not be able to buy everything she wanted so quickly."

"What can we do?" Rocana asked.

"First," Patrick replied, "I will take Caroline from the Castle as soon as her parents think she has retired for the night."

He was obviously working it out and Rocana said:

"That means about ten o'clock, which will give you nine hours before the Duchess will expect Caroline to be woken. It will be early as she is supposed to be married at a half after nine."

"I want longer than that."

"I cannot see how it is possible," Rocana replied, "but I am sure that if Caroline is missing and they guess what has occurred, the Duke will send his grooms riding in every possible direction to apprehend you."

That undoubtedly was what Patrick thought himself and she went on:

"You have to be married as quickly as possible, and that should be outside the County where the Parson would not be so familiar with the name of Brunt."

"I have thought it all out," Patrick said, "and the only way we have a real chance of being safe is if you will help us."

"Me?" Rocana questioned. "But of course! I will do anything you want."

"Do you mean that?" Patrick enquired in a somewhat strange voice.

"Of course I mean it," Rocana replied. "You know I love Caroline and she will never be happy with anybody but you."

"Very well," Patrick said. "What you have to do, Rocana, is to take Caroline's place and marry the Marquis!"

Rocana stared at him as if she thought she must have misunderstood what she had heard.

Then she gave a little cry before she exclaimed:

"What are you . . saying? How could I possibly do . . that?"

"It will not be easy," Patrick said, "but it is possible."

He paused as if he was thinking before he went on:

"You and Caroline are about the same height and you both have fair hair. The great difference between you is your eyes, but a bride is always supposed to look down, and besides you would be wearing a veil over your face."

"I . . I do not understand," Rocana said. "How can you have . . thought of anything so . . crazy?"

"It is not crazy if you think about it," Patrick said quietly. "The Duchess, who has eyes far sharper than the Duke's, will go ahead to the Church, and Caroline will come last with her father."

"Y . yes . . but. . ." Rocana began.

"If you contrive," Patrick went on as if she had not spoken, "that the Duchess does not see Caroline before she is dressed as a bride, I do not believe either the Duke or the Marquis when you reach the Church, will notice that you have taken her place."

Rocana's eyes were wide and her hands were clasped tightly together, but she did not speak as Patrick continued:

"Once you are married and legally the Marquis's wife, however much they may rage and scream there will be nothing they can do about it, and by the time they have sent the servants to find Caroline and me, we will be married."

Rocana put up her hands to pull off her riding-hat as if somehow it constricted her thinking.

Then she said:

"I cannot . . believe what you are . . saying to me!"

For the first time since they had met Patrick smiled.

"If you think it over, Rocana," he said, "you will not

only be helping Caroline, whom I know you love, but also yourself."

She looked at him in surprise, and he said:

"You may have no wish to marry the Marquis, but surely it would be preferable to living as you are now? Caroline has told me how you are continually abused because your father died in debt and your mother was French."

This was indisputable and Rocana made a little murmur which he took for one of agreement.

"Whatever happens in the future," he said, "the Marquis will have to look after you. Perhaps your 'magic' which Caroline has told me so often you use to see into the future, will tell you that this is the right thing for you as well as for us."

"I understand what you are .. saying to me," Rocana said, "but how could I possibly .. get away with such a .. deception? And if they .. expose me before I get to the Church, the Duchess will be so angry .. I think she .. might kill me!"

"Then you must make sure she does not find out until you are the Marchioness of Quorn!" Patrick said.

Then as if he thought he had been too frivolous, he put out his hand and took Rocana's.

"This is the only way you can help us, Rocana, and I feel it is a sort of poetic justice in return for the way in which the Duchess had treated you! I also believe your father would think it a good joke."

Almost as if Patrick had conjured him up, Rocana could see her father laughing, his eyes twinkling as he was saying:

"Serve them right! They deserve what is coming to them!"

It was an expression she had heard him use and she knew that if he was aware, as she was sure he was, of how unhappy she had been since coming to live at the Castle, he would want to save her.

She had thought last night when she went to bed, having sat up until nearly midnight sewing the garments the Duchess had left for her, that she could not bear to think of the future.

Because the Duchess hated her and was so spiteful she was sure that she definitely would prevent her from riding and reading.

Furthermore the only thing that had restrained her from punishing her physically in the past had been the presence of Caroline.

Rocana now had the feeling that once Caroline was married and no longer there the Duchess would slap her if she was annoyed and might even go further and beat her.

It was something she had threatened to do when she was very angry, but she would never have done so in front of Caroline. Rocana knew her cousin always had been a shield between herself and the Duchess's hatred.

So if Caroline was no longer there not only would she herself suffer, but Caroline also would be miserable and unhappy as the Marchioness of Quorn.

Rocana was aware that Patrick was waiting, just looking at her, his fingers tightening on hers which told her how tense he was and how urgently he was pleading with her to accept his suggestion.

Without realising it, she lifted her chin in a way which had been characteristic of her father when he was challenged by any particular difficulty and replied:

"I will do it . . but oh, Patrick . . you will . . have to . . help me!"

"I knew you would!" Patrick said in a tone of triumph. "Thank you, Rocana, thank you! And once Caroline and I are married, if things are too difficult you can always come to us."

"I . . I am frightened!" Rocana said, "not only of . . letting you down . . but of . . marrying the Marquis!"

"I agree he is rather frightening," Patrick replied. "At the same time, he is a gentleman and a sportsman, and I cannot believe that when you get to know him he will be any more formidable than the Duchess who terrified me!"

78

Rocana laughed, but it flashed through her mind that while the Duchess was, as Patrick said, terrifying, the Marquis would be her husband, and that was something it was almost impossible to contemplate.

"Now what we have to do," Patrick said in a practical tone, "is first of all to see that I have enough of Caroline's clothes for her to wear until I can buy her some more."

As if he thought that Rocana did not understand he added:

"You will have her new trousseau!"

"If I get away with my . . deception," Rocana murmured, "and . . go away with the . . Marquis!"

"You will be his wife," Patrick said firmly, "and whatever else happens, you must insist upon his taking you with him."

Rocana gave a gasp as if everything Patrick said made the future seem more and more complicated.

She did not speak and he went on:

"Could you possibly pack some of Caroline's clothes and make some excuse to the servants in the Castle for sending them away?"

Rocana thought for a moment. Then she said:

"As they all know she is having a complete trousseau, I could say that the Duchess instructed me to give everything she has worn for a long time to one of the Orphanages."

"Excellent!" Patrick exclaimed. "Get the footmen to put the trunks outside the back door tomorrow night and I will collect them. If I come at the time the servants usually have supper there is not likely to be anybody about."

"Suppose somebody sees you?" Rocana suggested.

"I will make sure they do not," Patrick replied. "Do not worry about me, Rocana, just pack the things you think Caroline will want."

"I will do that," Rocana promised.

"We will talk about this again tomorrow," Patrick said, "and I will work out every detail, but in the meantime, think what you can do to hide your eyes which is what will give you away, and of course there will have to be some explanation of your not being available as yourself, should the Duchess ask for you."

"I had not thought of that!" Rocana exclaimed.

Then she smiled.

"I know the answer to that problem at least."

"What is it?"

"Nanny will help me. She will come back from London with Caroline and I can say I am too ill to appear while she is dressing Caroline for the Church. I have already been told I am not to go to the wedding."

"Or the Reception?" Patrick asked.

"Of course not. You know I am supposed to be invisible."

"I cannot imagine anything more cruel than the way your father's daughter is treated, and apart from infuriating them by taking Caroline away, I want to see the Duchess get her just desserts when she realises that you are the Marchioness of Quorn!"

"I could not be more miserable than I should be at the Castle without Caroline," Rocana said in a low voice.

Patrick once again took her hand in his.

"I am not going to thank you, Rocana," he said. "All I can say is that I think you are very brave and your father would be proud of you."

Because of the sincere way in which he spoke Rocana felt the tears come into her eyes.

Her fingers tightened on his as she said:

"It cannot be more difficult than your competing with the Marquis in a Steeple-Chase and this time we will win!"

"We will win!" Patrick echoed.

. . . .

Rocana was unable to sleep when at last she went to bed on Saturday night having seen Patrick again in the morning.

He had been extremely encouraging and had rehearsed everything she had to do step by step, until almost as if it was written down in front of her, she could learn it by heart.

But she still felt terrified that she would fail and their whole plot would prove a disaster.

Caroliine had arrived home with the Duchess and Nanny at five o'clock and one look at her told Rocana how frightened and apprehensive she was.

The Duchess bustled into the Castle giving orders in a sharp voice and immediately finding fault with the flowers that had been arranged for the wedding.

Caroline ran upstairs and Rocana followed her.

They were both breathless by the time they reached the School-Room and as Rocana shut the door behind them Caroline asked:

"Patrick! What does he say?"

"It is all right. He will be waiting for you tonight at nine-thirty in the shrubbery by the back-door."

Caroline gave a little cry of joy.

"You are sure – you are really – sure he will be – there?"

"Absolutely sure," Rocana answered, "and I will tell you quickly what he has planned."

She drew Caroline to the window-seat because it was furthest from the door.

As she undid the ribbons of her bonnet and unclasped the cloak she wore over her thin gown Rocana told her in a whisper what Patrick had persuaded her to do.

"You will take my – place in the Church!" Caroline exclaimed. "I do not believe it!"

"Patrick says he must have at least that length of time to enable you to marry and reach the coast."

"Then you – will do it for me?" Caroline asked. "You will – really marry the – Marquis?"

"Patrick has persuaded me that it is the only possible way by which you can escape."

"Oh, Rocana, I am sorry! He is horrid and I hate him! I grow more frightened of him every time I see him!"

"Patrick insists that as far as I am concerned he cannot be more frightening than Aunt Sophie."

"Patrick is always right," Caroline replied, "and if you really will marry the Marquis I will thank you from the bottom of my heart, every day of my life!"

"I have promised that is what I will do," Rocana said, "and I only hope your wedding-gown will not be too .. tight for me!"

Caroline laughed, as Rocana wanted her to do, because they both knew that Rocana was the slimmer of the two and Caroline always complained that her own waist was less fashionable than hers.

"I suppose you will be expected to wear the family veil?" Rocana asked.

Caroline nodded.

"Mama kept saying all the way here that she hoped you would have the sense to get it ready and hang it up so that there are no creases in it."

"I have done that," Rocana said, "and fortunately the lace is very concealing."

"Supposing Mama sees you in the morning after I have gone?"

"That is where Nanny has to help us."

While Caroline was downstairs with her parents Rocana revealed the plot to Nanny.

Although she did not approve, since she would have liked 'her baby' as she called Caroline, to make a grand Social marriage, she knew better than anybody else that she would be happy only with Patrick.

"A nice lot of trouble I'm going to be in over this!" she said when Rocana had finished talking.

"You know Caroline wants you with her the moment she returns to England," Rocana replied, "and I am sure the best thing you can do is to go to Mr. Fairley's new house and wait for them there."

She then told Nanny what she had told Caroline: that Patrick now owned a very large house and estate in Oxfordshire which had been left him – together with a great deal of money by his Uncle.

Nanny was delighted by the news while Caroline had thought it unimportant compared with the fact that she was to marry Patrick tomorrow.

"We may have to stay away from England for a long time," she had murmured dreamily, "at least until we are quite certain that Papa cannot get the marriage annulled."

"I think he is unlikely to try to do that," Rocana said. "It would just make him and Aunt Sophie look foolish."

"Mama will want to punish me for running away, and if she can she will hurt Patrick."

Rocana thought that was very likely the truth, and everything therefore depended on her acting her part so well that Patrick gained enough time to take Caroline out of reach of her parents.

Soon after dawn she got out of bed, washed and started to arrange her hair in exactly the same style as Caroline had been wearing when she returned last night from London.

It was very becoming and quite different from the way she had done it in the past.

It took Rocana some time and she was still sitting in front of the mirror when Nanny came into the room.

"I thought you'd be awake," she said. "Did everything go all right last night?"

"Perfectly!" Rocana replied.

She told Nanny how she had taken Caroline down the back-stairs while the servants were away having their supper, and they had slipped out of the side door to find Patrick waiting for them behind the shrubbery.

He had a new Phaeton which he had already told Rocana he had purchased because it could travel so swiftly, and a superlative team of horses which had belonged to his Uncle.

There was a groom with him and he quickly took from Rocana Caroline's jewel-box and a case that contained a few things she had bought in London which she particularly wanted Patrick to see.

One of them, Rocana noticed with a smile, was a very beautiful nightgown and a négligée to match it, both trimmed with expensive lace.

"Patrick is going to buy you a new trousseau," she told Caroline, "and he already has all your best gowns with him which the household thinks are being taken to an Orphanage!"

Caroline laughed and exclaimed:

"You are both so clever! And I am delighted, dearest Rocana, for you to have my trousseau, which has cost Mama far more money then she intended to spend!"

There was still enough light in the sky when Patrick greeted Caroline for Rocana to see how happy they both were.

In fact, the radiance in their faces seemed to glow like starlight.

Caroline threw her arms around Rocana.

"Thank you, dearest!" she cried. "This could never have happened without you, and I shall be praying all through the night that everything will be all right tomorrow morning."

They had driven away and Rocana watched them disappear into the dusk at the end of the drive. She had then gone back into the Castle feeling that whatever happened to her, two people had found the ideal happiness which was like something out of a fairy-story.

She went to bed and tried to sleep because she knew it was the sensible thing to do.

But now the real test had come!

With Nanny going ahead to see there was nobody about she moved from her own bedroom into Caroline's.

Nanny then locked the door of Rocana's room and took away the key.

"I'm going to tell Her Grace you've got a streaming cold," she said, "and the last thing you wants is to come near Lady Caroline and for her to catch it!"

"That is sensible," Rocana agreed.

She got into Caroline's bed and Nanny said:

"I'll be back in half-an-hour to bring you a cup of tea. It's not likely Her Grace'll be about for another hour or so, so try to get some rest."

It was easier said than done and Rocana lay awake feeling cold and actually shivering with fear.

Because it was the only thing she could do she prayed both to God and to her father and mother for help.

"You were so happy," she said, "and I want to be happy too, but I shall never meet anybody here in the Castle just as a sewing-maid and being bullied by Aunt Sophie. Perhaps if I cannot marry for love, I might become friends with the Marquis. At least we have horses in common, if nothing else!"

It was however rather poor comfort, and she knew she was very apprehensive of what the Marquis would say when he found he had been deceived, if she actually got so far as having his ring on her finger.

She was praying and going over everything in her mind when Nanny came back, bringing her a cup of tea which Rocana sat up to drink.

Then Nanny drew back the curtains, leaving the blinds half-drawn and arranged Caroline's wedding-clothes ready for her to put on.

As they had both anticipated, about three-quarters of an hour later the door opened and the Duchess came into the room.

"Not up yet?" she said sharply. "It is time you began to dress. Your future husband has been insistent that we must not be late, and it would be a great mistake to start your marriage off on the wrong foot."

Rocana however did not reply. She just held a hand-kerchief to her eyes and the Duchess added crossly:

"What are you crying about? You will make your face look a mess."

Nanny moved quickly to the Duchess's side to say:

"I'd like to speak to Your Grace privately."

It seemed as if the Duchess might refuse, then reluctantly with a backward look at her daughter she went towards the door, and Nanny opened it for her.

Outside in the passage Nanny said:

"Don't upset her, Your Grace. She's just feeling

miserable at leaving home, but she'll be all right. I'll get her downstairs in time."

"What is she behaving like this for?" the Duchess enquired.

"Marriage is a step in the dark, Your Grace," Nanny said, "and Her Ladyship's always been very sensitive."

The Duchess snorted, but as if she realised that Nanny was talking sense she walked towards the staircase saying:

"Very well. Mind she is dressed in half-an-hour's time, then bring her to my room for me to fix the tiara on her veil."

"I think I'd better do that, Your Grace," Nanny said. "If she goes on crying as much as she's crying now, we'll have her in a state of collapse."

"I have never known her behave in such a ridiculous manner!" the Duchesss exclaimed.

"Leaving home with a strange man, Your Grace, is an ordeal for any young woman, an' Her Ladyship's little more than a child."

"Very well," the Duchess conceded, "You may come and fetch the tiara now, and I will let you know when I am leaving for the Church."

She proceeded down the stairs like a ship in full sail and Nanny followed her.

Rocana was not disturbed again until a footman knocked on the door to say the Duchess was leaving for the Church and Her Ladyship was to be downstairs in the Hall in five minutes time.

"I'll see she's not late," Nanny announced and the footman gave her an impertinent grin.

When Rocana was dressed in the beautiful wedding-gown chosen for Caroline and Nanny had put some finishing touches to her hair, it would have been difficult to know she was not her cousin, unless somebody had been able to see her eyes.

Because she was frightened her eyes were purple in their depths and had a strange mystic quality about them that was not wholly English.

Like Caroline, she too resembled the beautiful Lady Mary Brunt after whom they had both been christened.

Lady Mary had married her cousin who later became the 8th Earl of Brunt and fought in the wars under Marlborough with such distinction that he was created the first Duke of Bruntwick.

Lady Mary had gone to France with her husband and had ridden beside him on the battlefield.

She was reputed through her intelligence and quick wits to have directed one battle so well that it was successfully won against the French before Marlborough himself came up with reinforcements.

Because she was a legend in the Brunt family, every daughter born to the reigning Duke and his sons was given Mary as her first name.

Therefore, just as Caroline's name was prefixed with Mary, so Rocana had been christened 'Mary Rocana'.

This, as Patrick had already pointed out to her, would make her responses in Church easier than they might otherwise have been.

But her eyes would undoubtedly give her away to anybody who looked closely at her, and she had a very different aura from Caroline's.

She herself was not aware of it, but her mother had known of it and so had her father.

"It is something she had inherited from you, my darling," Lord Leo said to his wife, "and although it is difficult to put into words, it is the 'magic' I have always associated with you, as well as something spiritual which other women do not have."

"How could any daughter of yours not be an unusual and exceptional person?" Rocana's mother had asked tenderly.

"Or yours," Lord Leo replied.

But as she looked at her reflection in the mirror Rocana was only hoping that with her veil over her face and if she kept her eyes downcast – neither her Uncle, her Aunt or the Marquis would suspect that she was not Caroline.

"Now don't worry about anything," Nanny was saying as she took her towards the door. "People sees what they expects to see, and they're not expecting to see anybody but my baby beneath that veil."

"I . . I hope you are . . right," Rocana remarked with just a movement of her lips.

Nanny lifted the end of the veil which trailed behind her gown.

As the Wedding was to be a quiet one the Duchess had decided against a train which would have required bridesmaids or pages to carry it.

Instead the lovely white gown trailed a little way behind her, while the ancient Brussels lace veil billowed out gracefully when it was set down on the ground.

Nanny held it up as they went down the stairs and Rocana resisted an impulse to look about her and kept her eyes on the ground.

The Duke was waiting for her in the Hall, looking very resplendent with the Order of the Garter across his chest and a number of decorations on his cut-away coat with its long tails.

"Come along, come along!" he was saying sharply as Rocana descended. "We are due at the Church at nine-thirty, and we have less than three minutes to get there."

Rocana could not help thinking it would do the Marquis good to wait, but she knew it would be a mistake to say anything.

As she reached the bottom stair the Duke walked ahead out through the front door and down the steps to where a closed carriage was waiting.

The horses had wreaths of white flowers on their harness and the coachman had a bow of white satin ribbon attached to his whip.

The Duke got in first so that he was sitting on the far side of the carriage and Nanny made a great business of lifting in the veil.

After she had finished the footman laid a bouquet which had been arranged by the gardeners on the seat opposite them.

The carriage drove off and as Rocana sat with her head bent the Duke said testily:

"Nothing but rush, rush, rush! Typical of young people today! I would have liked you, Caroline, my dear, to have been married in the old-fashioned way with a proper wedding-breakfast to follow the ceremony."

He paused before he went on:

"But I was not consulted! Your mother arranged everything with your future husband, and if you ask me it is all quite unnecessary!"

Then as if he thought he should talk more intimately to his daughter he said:

"I shall miss you, Caroline. You have been a good girl. But I do not pretend I am not pleased you are marrying a man in such an important position and who is so well endowed with this world's goods. At the same time, Quorn is a difficult man and I dare say he will make a difficult husband!"

The Duke drew in his breath before he continued:

"Nevertheless, he is a gentleman, and he will do the right thing by you. If you take my advice you will not go prying into his private affairs. All young men have to 'sow their wild oats' and Quorn by all accounts has produced a whole harvest of them!"

The Duke gave a short laugh at his own joke, then thinking perhaps it was not very appropriate said:

"Well, here we are, and just you do what he wants, and no tears. No man likes a crying woman!"

As he finished speaking the door of the carriage opened and the footman jumped down from the box to help them alight.

Rocana did not hurry. She took the bouquet the flunkey handed to her, then reached out to rest her hand on her Uncle's arm.

They had to go a little way up the Church path to reach the porch and there were people from the village lining it.

Rocana did not raise her eyes, but she could hear them exclaiming at how beautiful she looked, and those in the front said as she passed:

"Good Luck, M'Lady!" "God Bless you, dearie!" "May you be very happy!"

She dared not look at them but just bowed her head a little to show her appreciation of their good wishes.

Then they had reached the porch and she could hear the organ playing softly.

The Duke stopped for a moment. Than as if he thought there was no point in waiting, he led her up the aisle.

As the wedding had been arranged in such a hurry, Rocana was aware there were only those of their relations who lived in the vicinity and a few friends and neighbours in the front pews.

She could hear the rustle they made as they turned round to watch her approach on the Duke's arm.

Although she did not even glance from under her eye-lashes she was aware that the Marquis was waiting for her at the Chancel steps.

Just for a moment it flashed through her mind that she was making a terrible mistake in tying herself irrevocably to a man she did not know and of whom everybody was afraid.

'I am crazy!' she thought and wondered if at the last moment she should run away.

She had a sudden vision of herself tearing down the aisle, throwing her bouquet to the ground.

Then almost as if it was a picture in her mind, she could see the Castle waiting for her like a prison.

Once the doors were closed on her the light outside would be shut out for all time and she would be incarcerated as if she were a Nun.

'Even the Marquis is better than that!' she thought, then was aware that she was standing at his side.

The Parson was their local Vicar because the Duchess had not, as she would have done had the wedding been a large one, asked the Bishop to perform the ceremony.

He began the service and somehow Rocana remembered at the right moment to have her bouquet taken from her.

As she gave her left hand to the Marquis she felt the strength of his fingers and knew that the vibrations coming from him were as strong and overpowering as she had known they would be if he touched her.

'He is frightening . . very frightening!' was all she could think as they made the responses which would make them man and wife.

"I, Titus Alexander Mark," he was saying, "take thee, Mary Caroline to my wedded wife, to have and to hold, from this day forward. . ."

Rocana could hear his voice, firm and authoritative ringing out in the quietness of the Church.

Then the Clergyman turned to her.

Because she wanted to give the Duke no possible grounds for annulling the marriage, she was determined to speak in a voice that was hardly audible.

" 'I, Mary Caroline, take thee. . .' he began.

After a perceptible pause and in a hesitating whisper Rocana echoed:

"I . . Mary . ."

She stumbled over the next word so that it was completely incoherent and went on a little louder:

". . . take thee . . Titus Alexander Mark to my wedded . . husband. . ."

Then the wedding ring was on her finger, and she knew that it was done.

She was married and, as the Parson said, no man could put them asunder.

The Register, presumably by the Marquis's order, so as not to waste time, was ready in the Chancel.

As the Marquis signed the book, Rocana threw back her veil, but pulled the sides of it around her and bent her head so low that she hoped it was impossible for anyone to see her face, especially with the large diamond tiara glittering above it.

Then she was walking down the aisle on her husband's arm, still with bent head and eyes downcast, to the sound of the Wedding March played loudly but not very well on the organ.

As they reached the porch there was a shower of rose-petals and rice, and the Marquis quickened his pace a little so that Rocana found her lace veil catching on the gravel path.

They however reached the carriage, to find, which she had not expected, that it had been opened while they were inside the Church.

Only as they started to drive away did she realise that this was in fact, a blessing.

Since the Church ceremony had begun, many more people had come from the village to line the drive up to the Castle and throw flowers and rice into the carriage as they passed.

This meant there was no need of any conversation, and Rocana turned away from the Marquis to wave at those waving to them, at the same time keeping her head down in case they should notice, as nobody else had, that she was not Caroline.

When the horses drew up outside the front door Nanny was waiting to lift up her veil at the back and to hurry her up the steps.

Only as she reached her bedroom did Rocana realise that she and the Marquis had not exchanged one word since they had become man and wife.

"Was it all right?" Nanny asked as soon as the door was shut behind Rocana held out her hand on which glowed the golden wedding-ring on her third finger.

"Thank God!" Nanny exclaimed. "I've been praying no one'd guess you were not who you appeared to be."

"Now I have to get away without Aunt Sophie realising it," Rocana replied.

"I doubt if she'll come upstairs," Nanny said, "but hurry, and I've lowered the lace on your bonnet."

Last night, when Nanny had unpacked Caroline's going-away outfit, she and Rocana found the high-brimmed bonnet was in the very latest fashion edged with a row of lace which acted almost like a veil.

It was very attractive and, Rocana thought, very glamorous. She also knew it would help to conceal her face, especially if she kept her head bent.

It was fortunate that neither she nor Caroline were tall. In fact they both measured only five foot five inches, and in her low slippers she had been aware that standing beside the Marquis her head only came up to his shoulder.

"I must arrange not to leave until the very last moment," she said to Nanny.

"There shouldn't be any difficulty now since His Lordship's in such a hurry to go," Nanny replied.

Rocana hoped she was right, and as she hurriedly changed her clothes for an elegant pale blue travelling-gown and cloak of the same colour she prayed there would be no sign of the Duchess.

Her prayers were answered because it was a footman who knocked on the door to say:

"His Lordship's compliments, M'Lady. He'd like to be leavin' in a few minutes."

Nanny replied:

"Very well. Will you bring upstairs a glass of champagne for Her Ladyship and a piece of wedding-cake? She'll not have time to join the others in the Banqueting Hall."

Again because of the haste with which the marriage was to take place, the Ball-Room had not been opened as was traditional for the Reception.

In fact, Rocana was certain there were so few guests at the wedding that even the Dining-Room would seem too large.

She knew it was impossible anyway for her to go there, and when the champagne was brought upstairs she sipped a little of it.

She found it impossible to eat anything because in her nervousness she felt quite sick.

She was however completely ready, and Nanny, just in case the Duchess should come upstairs, had drawn the blinds again.

"Here's your handkerchief, dearie," Nanny said, "and if Her Grace does appear I'll tell her you've

93

had another fit of crying."

"It is what I feel like doing," Rocana answered.

"Don't you dare!" Nanny said. "You've got to have your wits about you! Remember, the further you gets before he discovers who you are, the better it'll be for my baby."

"I have not forgotten that," Rocana said with a smile. "But I am not looking forward to the moment when he accuses me of being a liar and, I dare say, a crook!"

As she spoke she realised that Nanny was not listening, but was intent only on helping Caroline, who filled her whole world.

Rocana suddenly felt sorry for the old woman left alone to bear the brunt of the Duchess's inevitable rage.

Then she remembered that Nanny could leave and go to Caroline's new home, while if she had been discovered, she would have had to stay and endure recriminations and accusations for the rest of her life.

There was another knock on the door.

"His Lordship's in the Hall, M'Lady," a footman announced, "and says his horses're restless!"

Rocana gave a little laugh.

"And that is more important than anything else!" she whispered to Nanny.

"Her Ladyship's just coming," Nanny said to the footman. "Please suggest to His Lordship he gets into the Phaeton. Her Ladyship has no wish to be upset by long farewells."

The footman looked surprised, but sped down the stairs to give Nanny's message.

Again Rocana waited until she was quite certain that impatient, and doubtless irritated at the delay, the Marquis would be having difficulty in controlling his horses.

She saw this was in fact, the case when she reached the top of the stairs and saw her Uncle and Aunt were in the doorway, while the rest of the guests had grouped themselves on the steps outside.

As she descended she saw that the Marquis, undoubtedly by this time out of patience, had already climbed into the Phaeton and the grooms were at the heads of the leading horses who were very restless.

Rocana reached the Hall, then went to her Uncle's side.

He bent his head in an effort to kiss her beneath her bonnet and holding a handkerchief to her eyes she turned towards her Aunt.

"Goodbye, my dear," the Duchess said, "and stop crying! There is no need for it."

Rocana made no effort to reply but merely hurried down the steps amid a shower of rose-petals and rice.

Somebody helped her into the Phaeton, and with a cheer from the guests assembled on the steps the grooms stepped back from the horses' heads and they were off.

The Marquis crossed the bridge over the lake and drove down the drive at a speed which sent the dust billowing out behind them like a cloud.

Rocana settled herself comfortably, thinking as she did so that it was lucky it was such fine weather and they did not have to be confined to a closed carriage.

She knew that would have brought forward the inevitable moment when the Marquis would discover that he had married a stranger.

Then as they passed through the huge ornamented gates and out onto the dusty highway she thought with a sudden lift of her heart that she had done it!

It seemed unbelievable, but nobody had suspected for one moment that she was not Caroline!

Now the morning was drawing on, and it could still be some time before the Marquis realised the truth and doubtless learnt that Caroline was with Patrick. Even then nobody would have the slightest idea where they could be found.

It gave Rocana such a sensation of triumph that she felt as if she had suddenly come to life and that everything around her was fresh and green.

The sun was in fact, shining and while it was a very lucky sign for Caroline's Wedding Day, she hoped also a little of the luck would rub off onto her.

She was however aware that the last fence still lay ahead of her and it was likely to be not only difficult but perhaps dangerous.

For the moment however there was no risk that the Marquis would look at her closely, and they had driven for quite a long way before he said:

"I suppose I should apologise to you for insisting on everything having to take place in such haste. It would actually have been far easier if your mother had agreed to my suggestion that we should be married yesterday."

"I am quite . . content as things . . are," Rocana answered softly, hoping he would not recognise that her voice was different from her cousin's.

"I wonder if that is true," the Marquis said dryly. "I thought all women wanted to be married with a large number of bridesmaids and a huge Reception afterwards."

"That is what they may . . expect," Rocana replied, "but I have always thought it could . . prove very . . disappointing."

"Disappointing?" the Marquis asked curiously.

"I think one would always be conscious that the majority of the women in the congregation, when one married somebody like you, would be either jealous or . . envious."

She was speaking as she might have spoken to her father when they tried to cap each other's remarks and if possible to be amusing.

The Marquis did not reply for a moment. Then he said:

"I never thought of it before from a woman's point of view. From my own, I dislike shaking hands for hours on end, and listening to a lot of inane speeches apart from having to make one oneself."

Rocana laughed.

"But surely that adjective could not apply to Your Lordship?"

She thought as she spoke that she sounded a little sarcastic and was aware that the Marquis turned his head for a moment to look at her.

96

Fortunately her bonnet made it impossible for him to see her face, and she told herself she should be more careful.

But some little devil sitting on her shoulder whispered that as there was undoubtedly going to be a flaming row sooner or later, she had nothing more to fear.

Since she had been at the Castle she had never been allowed to have an intelligent conversation with anybody so she had missed the times when she and her mother had talked together on many serious subjects.

But more then anything else she had missed the times when she laughed with her father and they duelled with each other in words.

Because she had known he disliked stupid women and had always said how much they bored him, she would try to think of subjects she knew interested him.

She would then start a conversation just because she was aware they would both have a great deal to say to each other about it.

With the Marquis she felt that at least she could be provocative and she said:

"As we are neither of us likely to be married again we may as well make the best of it or perhaps that is the wrong expression . . where you are . . concerned."

She was aware that once again the Marquis was surprised.

"Why should you think that?" he asked.

"Because I heard when I was in London that you had no wish to be married, and were known as 'The Elusive Marquis'!"

For a moment there was silence. Then he laughed.

"I had not heard that before,"

That was not surprising, Rocana thought, as she had only just invented the phrase herself.

"Do you think it is a truthful assessment of what you were and what you want to be?"

Again she knew that he looked at her before he replied:

"I admit to nothing of the sort! When I asked you to marry me, I was of course anxious that you should do so."

97

"I am very flattered," Rocana said, "but I suggest it was not the 'love at first sight' over which the poets eulogise."

She paused and added

"I think it was Marlowe who wrote:

'*Who ever loved that loved not at first sight?*' "

The Marquis seemed to be concentrating on his horses and after a moment she went on:

"We met first at Almack's, and when we were dancing together I had the feeling you were . . resenting wasting your time with a . . débutante."

She remembered that was what Caroline had told her, and she thought if she was embarrassing the Marquis he certainly deserved it.

The more she thought about it, the more she considered the way in which he had insisted upon being married with such unseemly haste to be an insult.

And if she had wanted to greet the few friends who had come to the wedding or to say long and loving farewells to her parents, he had made it impossible.

"He may be frightening," she told herself, "but he is also abominably selfish and inconsiderate."

That thought somehow made things better and she was not as frightened of him as she had been.

She thought too that if Caroline had been here at this moment, she would have been trembling and very, very nervous of the man she had married.

"I will not be frightened of him if I can help it!" Rocana told herself. "If I have deceived him, then he deserved it! And I do not believe for one moment that he has thought of his wife as a woman who wants to be loved."

They were now driving very fast along a straight stretch of the road and it was therefore difficult to talk.

Rocana was glad that her bonnet fitted tightly and would not be blown off her head.

At the same time the dust was unpleasant, and she wondered what the Marquis would say if she asked him to drive more slowly.

But only when the road began to bend and twist and he was forced to drive a little slower did she say:

"You have not yet told me why you are in such a hurry to reach France. It must be something of the utmost . . importance."

"It is!" the Marquis said briefly.

He did not seem inclined to say any more, and Rocana wondered whether it concerned a lady who had red hair and green eyes.

Or perhaps, and it would not be surprising, one with quite different colouring.

CHAPTER FIVE

Rocana stirred and realised that somebody was pulling back the curtains.

She opened her eyes and could not imagine where she was.

Suddenly she realised she was in the Marquis's yacht and at the moment the ship was not moving.

Then as the Valet who had looked after her last night pulled back the curtains on the last porthole he turned round and Rocana exclaimed:

"It is morning!"

"Yes, M'Lady, and you've slept all night."

Rocana stared round the cabin, finding it difficult to believe that what he had said was true.

Then she remembered.

Looking back it seemed incredible that she had hardly exchanged more than a few words with the Marquis from the moment they reached the main roads.

They had travelled at what she thought was a phenomenal speed for over two hours after leaving the Castle, then drew into the yard of a large Posting Inn.

"We will stay here for exactly twelve minutes," the Marquis said.

Rocana was aware that it was well over an hour since he had last spoken to her and made no reply.

She merely climbed down from the Phaeton and found the Proprietor was waiting to take her to the bottom of the stairs where a chambermaid in a mob-cap escorted her up to a large bedroom.

There was another maid in attendance, and while she washed the dust from her face and hands they shook her cloak and removed what seemed an abnormal amount of dust from her bonnet.

She was as quick as she could be, but when she went downstairs again and was taken to a private parlour she found there only a servant, who she gathered was one of the Marquis's to attend to her.

"His Lordship's compliments, M'Lady," the man said, "and he's eaten and gone ter see ter th'horses."

He served Rocana with a delicious dish of cold roast duck which she was sure had been brought with them, and there was also a glass of champagne which because she was thirsty she drank gratefully.

She was aware that it must be well over the twelve minutes she had been allotted and hurried out to find that the Marquis was already seated in the Phaeton, holding the reins of his new team.

When late in the evening they reached the outskirts of Dover she realised how fantastic the Marquis's organisation was.

They had changed horses twice since luncheon, and at each place where the Marquis allowed her five minutes respite there was a glass of champagne waiting for her and something light to eat.

It was what the Duke would have called 'Rush, rush, rush, all the way', but to Rocana it was a joy because she knew that every minute that the Marquis did not question her identity meant that Caroline and Patrick were further away from the Castle and very much safer.

When they drove into Dover and turned down to the harbour, she saw as the Marquis drew his horses to a stand-still his yacht at the quayside and was very impressed by it.

It was very much larger than she had expected.

As soon as they walked up the gang-plank to where the Captain was waiting to welcome them aboard the Marquis having shaken hands asked abruptly:

"Has the luggage arrived?"

"Half-an-hour ago, M'Lord!"

"Good! Then put to sea, Captain Bateson."

"Very good, M'Lord!"

While the two men were talking a small man, who Rocana was to learn later was the Marquis's valet, asked her to come below.

She followed him and he showed her into a large, very comfortable cabin where one of her trunks was already lying open.

She saw that an evening-gown had been unpacked besides her night-things.

"I thought after all th' dust on th' road," the Valet said, "Your Ladyship'd like a bath."

"Thank you very much," Rocana replied.

She was indeed longing for a bath and knew it was a great luxury to have one aboard a ship.

She guessed she had been given the Master Cabin which was normally occupied by the Marquis, and it flashed through her mind that he might be intending to share it with her.

As this was something she had no intention of doing she thought apprehensively that this was the moment when she must face him with the truth.

However she lingered in the bath longer than she should have done, thinking that if she kept him waiting there was nothing he could do about it, aware they were already out to sea.

She had heard the anchor being drawn up and was aware the sails were billowing out in the wind.

It was easy to guess that as the yacht belonged to the Marquis it would be built for speed.

Then when Rocana came into the bedroom from the bathroom and saw her nightgown lying on the bed, she suddenly felt dizzy with exhaustion.

She had not slept the night before and although it had been an exhilarating experience to travel so fast behind team after team of four superlative horses, she felt as if her mind was still moving apart from the rocking of the yacht.

"I will just rest for a few minutes," she told herself.

The bed was very comfortable and her head seemed to sink into the soft pillow as if it was a cloud, and she knew no more. . . . .

. . . .

Now, sitting up in bed Rocana asked:

"Have we crossed the Channel?"

"Quicker than His Lordship's ever done before, M'Lady," the Valet said proudly, "and His Lordship asked me to give Your Ladyship his compliments and say if it's convenient he'd like to leave in an hour's time.'

The Valet walked towards the door as he was speaking and added:

"I'll fetch Your Ladyship's breakfast."

The steward must have been waiting just outside the door, for the Valet returned immediately and put a tray on the bed beside Rocana.

When she looked at it she realised she was hungry, and at the same time she was wondering what the Marquis had thought when she had not appeared to dine with him, but had slept through the night.

She supposed while she was eating that the same rush as yesterday would take place today.

She was certain of one thing: the Marquis would not wish to delay his departure for Paris by having a long conversation with her which would be inevitable once he was aware that she was not Caroline.

'It will be better to face that after we reach Paris,' Rocana thought.

She had been right in thinking that the rush would be repeated, and when she came up on deck the Marquis was already on the quay with another Phaeton and another team of horses.

She was to learn later that he had sent his own horses and grooms ahead several days ago and that the luggage had left as soon as they docked.

The trunk that had been in her cabin had been

removed so quietly that she had not been disturbed, and the Valet had left her the clothes she had worn on the previous day.

He also provided her with a chiffon scarf.

"I thought Your Ladyship 'd find it useful," he said. "The dust on the French's roads be worse than ours, an' there's a bit of a wind at the moment."

Rocana thanked him, tied the chiffon scarf over her bonnet and round her chin.

This helped to conceal her face even better than before, and she thought how well everything was going.

Only when she saw the glint of her gold wedding-ring did she ask herself if everything that was happening could really be true. Was she in fact in a strange dream from which she could not awaken?

The roads to Paris, after they had left the twisting outside Calais, were straight, and there was not half so much traffic as there had been in England.

The Marquis's horses were fresh and covered the first two hours at what Rocana was sure was a record speed.

Then there were the same arrangements as had been made the previous day.

A quick luncheon at noon which the Marquis ate before she came down the stairs, and at the other places where they changed horses, there was champagne and a delicious *croissant* or a *pâtisserie* which was mouth-watering.

Again it was impossible to have any conversation for the Marquis was concentrating on his horses and the wind seemed to blow the words from Rocana's lips.

Only as they reached the outskirts of Paris and she had her first sight of the tall houses with their grey shutters did she realise that she was very tired.

She thought if she had to have it out with the Marquis tonight she would be too tired to have her wits about her and, what was more, if he was angry with her she might easily burst into tears.

"I will not tell him anything tonight," she told herself, "for the simple reason that he is inhuman!"

She knew Caroline would never have stood up to the demands of the journey as well as she had, and the more she thought about the arbitrary way in which he had insisted on marrying in such a hurry, the more she considered it an insult.

Women were human beings and most of them would have expected that the Marquis should at least make a pretence of having some sort of affection for the woman who now bore his name.

'It is inhuman of him to be so selfish and positively cruel,' Rocana decided.

She was determined that somehow she would make him aware of his short-comings when he accused her of hers.

But not tonight. That would be too much.

They travelled through small twisting streets, then came to some wider ones which told Rocana they were nearing the centre of the city.

The Marquis drove into the courtyard of what was the most impressive-looking house she had seen so far, drew a gold watch from his waistcoat pocket and said in a tone of satisfaction:

"Eleven hours, ten minutes!"

In a voice that did not sound like her own Rocana, because she was curious, managed to ask:

"What is the French record?"

"Twelve hours!"

There was no doubt that he was delighted with himself, but as Rocana stepped down onto the pavement she found her legs were unsteady.

In the Hall, a servant in resplendent livery, who she guessed was the Groom of the Chambers, welcomed her to Paris.

He then led her up a magnificent carved gilt and ebony staircase along a passage hung with fine pictures to what she guessed was a State Bedroom.

"Is this the Marquis's own house?" she asked.

105

"His Lordship purchased it three years ago from the *Duc* de Greville, *Madame*," the Groom of the Chambers replied, "and now we are very honoured to have *Mi'Lor* our Master."

The bedroom looked very romantic with a painted ceiling and white and gold walls inset with silk damask panels of Boucher blue.

Rocana thought it was a perfect background for her fair hair.

But she felt so tired that she knew she would sleep on a hay-stack just as well as in the huge gilt-carved and satin-draped bed which stood in an alcove.

"This is your *femme de chambre, Madame*," the Groom of Chambers was saying.

A young woman turned from the wardrobe where she had been hanging up Caroline's gowns which had just been unpacked from one of her trunks, and cursied.

"Her name is Marie," he continued, "and I hope she'll give Your Ladyship every satisfaction."

"I am sure she will," Rocana replied, "and as I am very tired, Marie, I would like to go to bed immediately."

She was speaking in French and Marie exclaimed:

"*Milady* speaks our language like a Parisian!"

"*Merci*," Rocana replied.

She wanted to add that she was half-French, but thought it was a piece of information which if it reached the Marquis's ears would certainly surprise him.

Instead she said to the Groom of the Chambers:

"Please express to *Monsieur le* Marquis my regret that I am unable to dine with him tonight, but it has been a long journey and I am exceedingly fatigued!"

"I am sure *Monsieur le* Marquis will understand," the Groom of the Chambers replied.

He left the room and although it was exciting to be able to converse in her mother's language in Paris, as she had always longed to do, Rocana let Marie undress her in silence and got into bed.

She was asleep before the maid left the room and although she had the idea that later some supper was brought she just turned away and went on sleeping.

It was however very different the next morning when Rocana awoke.

She knew it would be expected of her to ring the bell for a maid instead of jumping out of bed and pulling back her own curtains.

It was only a few minutes before Marie came into the room.

When she opened the shutters the sunshine came flooding in and in the daylight the room looked even more beautiful than it had at night.

"You are rested, *Madame*" Marie enquired.

"What is the time?" Rocana asked.

"Nearly noon, *Madame*."

Rocana gave a little laugh.

"I have never slept so long in my life before!"

She knew as she spoke that she had never been on such a gruelling journey before either.

At the same time, her exhaustion had been accentuated by her anxiety and apprehension over her marriage, and there had also been the nerve-wracking days before Caroline returned from London and her final agreement to Patrick's crazy idea that she should marry the Marquis.

It seemed incredible that everything had happened exactly as they planned. By now Caroline would be safely married and she herself was a wife of three days standing.

Marie brought her some coffee and while she was sipping it Rocana asked a little tentatively:

"Where is *Monsieur*?"

"*Monsieur le Marquis* has gone out, *Madame*, and he asked me to tell you that it will be impossible for him to return until late this afternoon."

Rocana was not surprised, but she did not say anything and Marie continued:

"He hoped *Madame* would amuse herself, and there

is a carriage available should one be needed."

Rocana lay back with a little sigh against the pillow.

"I think I would just like to rest," she said, "and also have something to read."

"I will fetch the newspapers, *Madame*," Marie said, "and there are books in the *Boudoir*, if *Madame* would care to choose one."

As soon as Marie left the room Rocana jumped out of bed and went through the communicating door which she was sure led into the *Boudoir*.

She was not mistaken and it was an extremely beautiful room decorated in the same elaborate manner as her bedroom, again with a painted ceiling and with pictures by famous artists.

To her delight there was a book-case of inlaid wood with glass doors which contained a great many works by French writers.

Some were books she and her mother had heard of and discussed but were not obtainable in England.

She hesitated as to which to read first, and finally picked three volumes which she took back to bed.

Marie brought her luncheon which was far more delicious than anything she had ever eaten in England.

She admitted her mother had been right in claiming that French food was the best in the world.

At the same time, while she was eating she was reading, and it was only quite late in the afternoon that she realised that as a wife she should be up, dressed and ready to greet her husband when he returned.

She was just about to ring for Marie when the maid came into the room to say:

"A message from *Monsieur le Marquis, Madame*, he has been unavoidably detained and will not be with you until dinner-time. He asks your forgiveness and hopes that you will dine with him at half after seven."

'That solves one problem,' Rocana thought.

She would not have to change twice, and because she did not want to think about what lay ahead she went back to reading her book.

Marie however prepared a bath for her an hour before dinner was due and informed her at a quarter to seven that the Marquis had returned.

Rocana wondered a little cynically if the lady who had prevented him from returning home was as alluring as the one with red hair and green eyes.

Then she told herself that those were not the sort of thoughts a bride should have.

"Bride or no bride," she said to herself, "this is a very unusual and certainly original honeymoon!"

She wanted to laugh about it, but even while she tried to tell herself it was amusing she was conscious of something heavy like a stone in her breast which she knew was fear of what lay ahead.

To give herself 'Dutch Courage' as her father would have said, she choose what she thought was one of the prettiest of the many gowns the Duchess had bought in London.

It was white which she thought was very appropriate for a bride, and embroidered all over with small diamanté which glittered like dew-drops.

It was also ornamented around the hem with lilies-of-the-valley and the same flowers encircled her bare shoulders.

A very high waist, Rocana noticed, was still fashionable, but now the gowns were no longer straight and shapeless, but worn with a small corset which made her waist seem even tinier than it was naturally.

Marie arranged her hair and insisted that she wore a little imitation diamond coronet on it which gave her a sparkle like a halo.

Rocana remembered that Caroline had a real diamond coronet, and she wondered if the Marquis would notice that hers was imitation.

The one she had worn on her wedding-day had belonged to the Duchess and of course had been left behind, and she thought a little wistfully that with the exception of her wedding-ring she owned nothing of value.

If the Marquis in his fury at having been deceived turned her out she would have not a penny of her own and nothing she could sell.

Then she told herself it was something he was unlikely to do because it would cause a scandal.

If, however, he should do so – and she was certain he could be ruthless when it suited him – she would have to find her mother's family.

Her mother had written to them after hostilities had ceased and had been planning that when things had settled down and they could afford it, she and her father would go to Paris.

Rocana had been so distraught by her mother's death that the contents of her home had been put in store by the Duke, and she had not taken with her to the Castle the addresses which she now knew would be useful.

It now also seemed rather foolish that she had not written to her French relatives.

One of the reasons was that the Duchess had forbidden her to communicate with what she still called 'the enemy', and any letters for France would undoubtedly, if seen, have been confiscated or destroyed.

"They are somewhere in Paris," she told herself, "and if the worst comes to the worst I can try to find them."

As she walked very slowly down the stairs she had a feeling that it might indeed be necessary, because 'the worst' was waiting for her.

A flunkey dressed in the resplendent uniform she had noticed when she arrived escorted her across the Hall, in which there was some very fine statuary, and opened the door of what she anticipated would be the Salon.

There were two huge crystal chandeliers shimmering with light although the curtains over the windows were not yet drawn. The sun had set, but the sky was still aglow with colour.

Then as everything seemed to swim in front of her

eyes, Rocana was conscious that standing at the far end of the Salon, looking elegant in a way she had never seen before was her husband.

If the Marquis was overpowering and magnificent in his riding-clothes and the clothes he had worn when driving, he looked even more impressive in knee-breeches, while his white frilled cravat made him seem even taller and more imperious than ever.

Slowly, because she knew this must be the moment of revelation, Rocana walked towards him, holding her head high, her chin lifted a little.

When she drew nearer to him the Marquis said:

"Good-evening, Caroline! I feel I have a great number of apologies to make to you, and I can only hope that now you are less exhausted and ready to hear them."

The manner in which he spoke was very pleasant, and he turned as she reached him towards the table on which there was a bottle of champagne in a silver ice-cooler.

"I think what we should do first," the Marquis went on, not waiting for Rocana's reply, "is to drink to our happiness – something we omitted to do on our wedding-day."

He poured out two glasses of champagne as he spoke and picking up the first one handed it to Rocana.

As she took it from him he looked down at her and she saw him stiffen.

He stared at her until gradually a look of astonishment came into his eyes.

Then in a voice which was very different from the one in which he had been speaking to her before he exclaimed:

"You are not Caroline!'

"No."

There was silence before the Marquis asked:

"Then who are you, and why are you here?"

"I am . . your wife."

The Marquis drew in his breath.

Then before Rocana could reply he said:

"You are the girl I met in the stables and who controlled *Vulcan!*"

"Yes, I am . . Rocana."

"And you say you are my wife?"

"Y. yes."

The Marquis for the moment seemed bereft of all speech. Then like a pistol-shot his voice rang out.

"What the Devil is going on? And what do you mean by being here in Caroline's place?"

Rocana's fingers tightened on the glass of champagne she held and she managed to answer:

"C. Caroline was . . in love with . . somebody else."

"Then why was I not told?"

"Her mother and father . . insisted that she should . . m. marry you."

The Marquis looked away from Rocana for the first time and picked up his glass of champagne.

He drank from it as if he needed its sustenance. Then he said:

"I think, Rocana, you have a great deal of explaining to do!"

"May I . . sit down?"

The Marquis made a gesture with his hand and Rocana seated herself on the sofa.

Her legs were trembling and she felt she was unable to stand.

Her hands were trembling too and she clutched the glass very tightly as if clinging to a life-line to save her from drowning.

She realised that the Marquis was waiting, and after a moment she said in a small, hesitating little voice:

"Caroline . . has . . eloped with the man she . . l. loves . . and it was essential that they should have. .time. .to get away so I . . took her place. . ."

"You took her place and married me!" the Marquis exclaimed. "I presume it is legal?"

"I . . think so."

112

"You made your vows as Mary – I remember that."

"I was christened 'Mary Rocana',"

"You resemble Caroline, so I presume you are some relation?"

"We are cousins."

"I recall now your telling me your name was Brunt. There appeared to be some mystery about you."

"The mystery," Rocana replied, "was because the Duchess hated my father and my mother."

She saw as she spoke the Marquis look at her cynically and she knew he thought she was trying to make excuses for her behaviour.

She therefore lapsed into silence and after a moment he said:

"You are very plausible as to why you married me, but I suspect the real reason was that you wished to become a Marchioness."

Rocana's chin went up proudly.

"Actually that is not true," she replied. "Patrick persuaded me it was the only way that he and Caroline could get away safely, since there was so little time between her return from London and the hour you wished the wedding to take place."

She thought the Marquis was not convinced and went on:

"If it had not all been such a rush and Caroline had returned earlier in the week, she could have eloped on Friday or Saturday, and there would have been no need for me to take her place."

The Marquis frowned as if he was following her train of thought before he said:

"Nevertheless you were not reluctant to do so!"

"For me it was a way of escape from being incarcerated like a prisoner in the Castle and forced to be nothing but a servant, or rather a sewing-maid, to my Aunt!"

"Do you expect me to believe that?"

"Whether you do or do not, it is still the truth."

"In fact you are insinuating that I was the better of

113

two evils!" the Marquis said sarcastically.

"That was what I was about to say myself," Rocana agreed. "I assure you, My Lord, I had no wish to marry you as a . . man!"

"Why not?"

"I . . I find you very . . frightening . . and also entirely self-centred."

"Self-centred?" the Marquis questioned.

"Certainly! You decided to marry Caroline because it suited you for reasons of which she was well aware. But she was not consulted in the matter and you just assumed she would be as delighted as the Duchess was."

She knew as she spoke that she had scored in a way which the Marquis had not expected, and after a moment he replied:

"I suppose, now I think about it, it was somewhat arbitrary!"

"It was quite unforgivable that Caroline should be treated as a chattel to be handed over to you by her parents without her having a chance to express her views about it."

She paused before she conceded:

"Actually, whatever you did, she would have disagreed, but that is beside the point."

"I have always understood that young girls' marriages were arranged for them," the Marquis observed, as if he must defend himself, "and that they were delighted to accept the highest bidder!"

Because he sounded so surprised that he might have got it wrong, Rocana gave a little laugh before she answered:

"Girls turn into women, and I doubt if Your Lordship would have treated any of the lovely ladies you have courted in London in such an inhuman manner."

The Marquis walked to the table to pour himself another glass of champagne.

He glanced at Rocana's glass as he did so and seeing that it was still three-quarters full he drank a little

114

from his own glass before he said:

"Then what do you suggest we do about this mess?"

"I suppose you will have to notify the Duke sooner or later that you . . married the . . wrong bride."

"Do you think he may not be aware of it already?"

"They may be wondering at the Castle what has happened to me, but I doubt if it will occur to them that you are not married to Caroline."

"And what do you think they will do about you?"

Rocana gave a little shrug of her shoulders.

"The Duchess will be delighted to be rid of me, but she will undoubtedly think it strange that I should run away without any money, and without even one of the horses!"

"Do you really mean that she hates you? But why should she?"

"I can answer that quite easily," Rocana said. "My father died in debt, and my mother was French!"

"French?" the Marquis repeated. "I suppose that accounts for your eyes."

Rocana gave a little laugh.

"I was afraid they would give me away sooner or later!"

"If Caroline is your cousin," the Marquis said as if he was working it out for himself, "then you are Lord Leo's daughter!"

"You knew my father?"

"I admired him very much!" the Marquis replied. "He rode magnificently, and now I understand how you inherited your gift of managing horses."

"Papa was wonderful with any horse, however wild."

"As I know you are."

Rocana smiled.

"I thought perhaps we . . would have one thing in . . common . . at any rate!"

The Marquis stared at her.

"Are you intending to continue with your impersonation of my wife?"

"It is not an impersonation," Rocana replied. "We are married, and although it may make you very angry .. as it is entirely legal .. I do not think there is much you can do .. about it!"

The Marquis put his glass down on the mantelpiece and turned away from her to look down at the empty fireplace which had been filled with flowers.

"I am not only angry," he said, "but I am also bewildered. I see that you and Caroline have made a complete fool of me, and that is hardly something I enjoy."

"I should have thought," Rocana said slowly, "the only possible way that you can avoid looking a fool is to make everybody think that you knew exactly what you were doing .. and that you married me .. deliberately."

"Why should I do that?"

"Because you want to save your face."

It was a point Rocana had only thought of at that moment, but it seemed to her logical.

When the Marquis turned to look at her in surprise she knew he was quick-witted enough to understand exactly what she was saying.

"You could say," she went on before he could speak, "that Caroline told you when you proposed to her that she was wildly in love with Patrick Fairley, and she begged you to pretend that she had accepted your offer in order to prevent her father and mother from forbidding her ever to see Patrick again."

Rocana spoke reflectively as the fiction of what happened seemed to unfold almost magically in front of her eyes.

"What nobody knew except ourselves," she went on, "was that you and I had met by chance before the Steeple-Chase and had fallen head-over-heels in love at first sight!"

She looked at the Marquis, then away again before he could say anything.

"It was therefore your clever idea that I should take Caroline's place in Church and that was why you were so insistent that the wedding must take place in such

116

a rush, so that no one should recognise me at the Reception!"

The Marquis stared at her, then quite unexpectedly he put back his head and laughed.

"I do not believe it!" he said. "This cannot be happening! I am dreaming!"

"I have thought I was dreaming," Rocana said, "ever since I agreed to take part in what I was quite certain would be a disastrous charade."

"And you really think anybody will believe such a fantastic tale which might have come out of 'The Arabian Nights'?"

"I cannot see it is any more fantastic than your insisting on marrying a girl you had only spoken to three times, and breaking every record in travelling from England to Paris on what is supposed to be a romantic honeymoon!"

The Marquis laughed again. Then he said:

"I suppose I should tell you why I was in such a hurry!"

"I admit to being very curious," Rocana answered, "and also why your engagement had to be so short, and you had to be married in such a rush."

She saw the Marquis's expression change as if this was something he had no wish to tell her.

But at that moment dinner was announced, and as she rose he offered her his arm and they walked slowly down the passage which led them to an attractive Dining-Room with the walls covered with what Rocana recognised was priceless tapestry.

There was a huge gold candelabra in the centre of the table with eight candles in it.

There were also a number of gold ornaments and gold goblets, the bases of which were decorated with a profusion of green orchids.

"How pretty!" Rocana exclaimed as she sat down.

"I regret they are not the traditional colour for a bride," the Marquis said, "but I was told they had just come into bloom in my greenhouses, and I thought you

117

would appreciate them more than rather mundane white carnations."

"Perhaps this colour is more appropriate."

"If you are suggesting that it is unlucky for me, you are wrong," the Marquis answered. "Green is one of my racing colours, the other is black."

"And you certainly have been lucky where your horses are concerned."

"I cannot complain," the Marquis said complacently, "although I did not beat that young man who challenged me at the last moment in the Steeple-Chase. I think you said his name was Patrick Fairley."

"I was praying he would beat you," Rocana said, "because it would have been an omen of good luck."

"Now I understand why he was so anxious to do so," the Marquis remarked.

Rocana gave a little sigh.

"It was a very exciting race, and I never thought Patrick would have a chance. But now he has won in a different way, and I hope you are sporting enough to wish him luck."

"I should have thought the same applied to me!" the Marquis said mockingly.

Rocana did not protest, but raised her glass and said:

"To Patrick, who has won a very special trophy, despite all the odds against him."

The Marquis raised his glass and drank. Then he said:

"I think really you should toast me as well, but to spare your blushes I will ask you to do that later."

It took Rocana a moment to realise that he was insinuating that he had won her, and was being extremely cynical about it.

Instead she said:

"The servants will be coming in soon with the next course, and I had hoped you were going to tell me why you were in such a rush to reach Paris."

"Of course," the Marquis agreed, "and the explanation is really quite simple: the Prince Regent asked me to buy privately on his behalf five extremely fine pictures, and I was obliged to do so today because tomorrow they were to be put on public sale."

"Pictures!" Rocana exclaimed. "That is something I did not expect!"

"What, as a matter of interest, did you think was the reason for such haste?"

Rocana thought perhaps she should not answer him. Then she said defiantly:

"If it was not a horse, and I thought you had enough of those, it could only be a . . woman!"

The Marquis looked at her as if he could not believe anything so small could be so impertinent.

Then he said:

"I can see, Rocana, that you are not in the least what I expected a young, inexperienced and unsophisticated *débutante* to be like."

"I am sorry if I disappoint you," Rocana replied, "but I have not been allowed to be a *débutante*, and actually I am nineteen, a year older than Caroline."

"And you have, I gather, accumulated quite a lot of knowledge in that extra year!"

The Marquis was again mocking her, and she said:

"Any knowledge I have, I can assure you comes entirely from books, for just as you did not meet me at the Castle, I have not been allowed to meet anybody else."

Her voice dropped as she went on very quietly:

"Ever since my father and mother died I have been kept in the background, snubbed, abused and punished. So if I am now behaving somewhat over-exuberantly, you must excuse me for feeling like a bottle of champagne that has just been uncorked."

The words seeming to tumble from her lips made the Marquis laugh.

"I have seen your imagination at work, Rocana, and I cannot help thinking this is another example of it."

"You must believe what you want to believe,"

119

Rocana replied, "but I invariably, whenever possible, tell the truth."

"Except when you are disguising yourself as somebody else!"

"There are of course exceptions to every rule."

"You are either very clever or very stupid," the Marquis said, "and I am anxious to separate the wheat from the chaff, or rather the truth from the lies!"

Rocana had realised as they dined – and she thought it was something new that the Marquis had introduced – that having served them, the servants left the room.

When he was ready for them to change the plates and bring on the next course he rang a small gold bell which stood in front of him.

Now they were alone, and Rocana said:

'What I can tell you, and I really am speaking the complete truth is that Caroline was terrified of you and hated you! I too am .. frightened of you and, although I do not hate you, I think you are a very unusual and difficult man."

As the Marquis did not reply she added:

"Now I think of it, that is what my Uncle said to me on the way to the Church, that you were difficult, and that I just had to do what you told me to do."

"Do you mean to do that?"

"It depends on what orders you give me," Rocana answered. "I have seen in the last few days how efficient you are, how everything you do is planned down to the last detail, and that is why I would prefer to know what to expect rather than speculate and be afraid."

The Marquis was silent for a moment. Then he said:

"You keep telling me how frightening I am. Is that really true?"

Rocana stared at him wide-eyed before she said:

"Surely you must be aware that everybody is frightened of you, except perhaps for the beautiful women who try to entice you, although I suspect really they are frightened of you too! Your grooms when they were at the Castle told me you frightened them."

The Marquis looked at her when he said:

"I suppose one can never see one's-self through other people's eyes. I know I am efficient. I like things around me to be perfect, but I did not think I controlled people by fear rather than by respect."

"I think what you are really saying," Rocana said, "is that you want them to admire you, and they do, even when they disapprove of your behaviour."

"What do you know about me?" the Marquis asked. "You tell me you have been incarcerated in the Castle. Had you ever heard of me before I met Caroline?"

"Of course I had heard of you!" Rocana replied. "I had heard of your successes on the race-course and as a pugilist, and of the duels you have fought and won, and of course of your many, many love-affairs!"

She spoke quite lightly, for the moment carried away by the novelty of talking freely to a man as she had talked to her father and mother, which was something she had not been able to do since they had died.

Then the Marquis suddenly brought his clenched fist down on the table, making the plates rattle and the glasses jump.

"How dare you!" he exclaimed. "How dare you speak to me like that! What do you know of my life? Who could have talked to you about me when it could not have concerned you?"

He almost shouted the words at her and for a moment Rocana could only stare at him, her eyes seeming to fill her whole face before as he waited for her reply she managed to say:

"I. I am . . sorry . . I spoke. .without thinking . . and I know now . . it was very . . rude of me."

Because she was humble and apologetic the anger went out of the Marquis's eyes and he said in a different tone:

"Now I *have* frightened you, and that is a mistake. You have been frank with me, Rocana, which is some-

121

thing I should have expected from you, although I do not often receive it from anybody else."

Rocana looked blindly at the orchids on the table.

"It was . . rude of me," she said, "but . . I have never been . . alone with . . anybody like . . you before."

Unexpectedly the Marquis put out his hand palm upwards towards her.

"Forgive me," he said. "You took me by surprise and I forgot how young you are."

Reluctantly, because he had upset her, Rocana slowly put her hand in his.

His fingers closed over hers and once again she was aware of his strength and the vibrations she had felt in the Church.

"I think, Rocana, we must make a pact," the Marquis said quietly.

"A . . pact?"

"That we will always speak frankly without either of us taking offence. We must try to make this strange and what for the moment seems quite ridiculous marriage of ours work."

CHAPTER SIX

Because the servants were now continually in the room Rocana had no further chance of talking intimately to the Marquis until dinner was finished.

Then they moved to the Salon and as he seated himself comfortably in an armchair Rocana without thinking sat down on the hearth-rug in front of the fireplace.

It was something she was so used to doing at the Castle when she was talking to Caroline, and previously when she was at home, with her parents, that she did not realise it might be unconventional in her new position.

The Marquis however did not say anything. He merely looked at her with her elegant gown billowing round her, its diamanté making her appear like a flower after the rain.

Then he said:

"Now let us talk sensibly about ourselves."

"I thought that was what we had been doing," Rocana replied.

"There are a great many things to decide," he said. "The first is when do you wish me to communicate with your Uncle and Aunt?"

Rocana gave a little cry.

"Not yet! Please . . not yet . . I want to be absolutely sure that Caroline is safe and also. . ."

She paused.

"And also?" the Marquis prompted.

Rocana hesitated for words.

"I . . I was wondering if you were . . quite certain you would . . keep me as your . . wife."

"And if I do not?" the Marquis asked. "What would you do?"

"It sounds rather . . grasping," Rocana said in a small voice, "but as I have no . . money I would have to ask you to give me . . enough so that I could go away and hide . . somewhere where Aunt Sophie could not . . find me."

She paused before she said in a voice that was very revealing:

"I could not bear to go . . back to the Castle knowing how she would . . punish me for . . deceiving her . . and you."

"Then that is certainly something you must avoid," the Marquis said. "I did suggest at dinner we should try to see if it is possible for our marriage to work."

"Do you . . really mean . . that?"

"I seldom say something I do not mean," the Marquis replied. "I admit that at first I wondered how I could extricate myself from the position in which you have put me, but I see there really is no way out of it without a scandal."

"I knew you would . . hate that!" Rocana said in a low voice.

"I would dislike it very much indeed," the Marquis answered, "and I will therefore agree to your plan, and say I married you because I wished to do so."

Rocana's eyes lit up.

'That would be . . wonderful for Caroline and it would save her . . I am sure, from her father and mother trying to . . get their marriage annulled."

"Then her future is settled," the Marquis said. "Now what about ours?"

There was silence. Then Rocana replied:

"As you have been so kind, I will try to be as . . unobtrusive as . . possible."

"What do you mean by that?"

"I mean," she said hesitatingly, "that as I know you

124

are . . in love with . . somebody else . . you will obviously want to . . spend as much time as . . possible with her."

"Who said I was in love with somebody else?" the Marquis asked angrily.

Rocana looked at him, a little apprehensively as she said:

"Caroline was told in London by quite a number of people that you were marrying in such haste because you had become involved with a very beautiful lady with red hair and green eyes."

She was silent before she added:

"They said your . . association with her might cause a . . diplomatic incident . . and so you . . decided to be . . married."

As she spoke she was aware that the Marquis had stiffened and she was sure that his temper was rising.

At the same time she knew it would be better if they were frank from the very beginning and she went on quickly:

"I . . I therefore . . as obviously I would not be upset by anything you do . . would not intrude when you wish to be . . alone with any lady in whom you are . . interested . . and perhaps we can become . . friends."

There was silence. Then the Marquis said:

"That is not the sort of marriage I was thinking of."

Rocana looked at him quickly.

"You . . you cannot mean that we should . . really be . . man and wife?"

"Why not?"

Rocana's eyes widened as if she could not believe what she had heard. Then she answered:

"I do not know what . . two people do when they . . make love . . but I know that for Caroline . . who adores Patrick . . it would be . . wonderful!"

She paused before she went on:

"But as you do not . . love me . . and I do not . . love you . . it would be . . wrong . . very wrong."

"But we are married, Rocana!" the Marquis said quietly.

"Only by mistake from your point of view, and although I am .. thrilled by your horses .. and your pictures .. that is .. different from being .. attracted to you as .. a man!"

There was a twist to the Marquis's lips as he said:

"Frankness is something I have not experienced before, Rocana, in my relationships with women."

"Please .. I am trying not to be .. rude or difficult..." Rocana said pleadingly, "but I must try to make you .. understand that ours is a .. different marriage from what you expected, and I .. wanted."

"I suppose every bride wants to be in love!" the Marquis remarked.

He made it sound as if it was something reprehensible and for a moment Rocana forgot to be humble and said:

"Of course she does! How could it be otherwise? Why should she be .. forced to marry a man because he is rich and important? It is wrong! It is against .. everything that God .. intended."

"And yet you married me," the Marquis insisted, "to save Caroline and yourself."

"I .. told you .. that."

"Then I suppose, in the circumstances, you do not think you owe me anything?

Rocana looked puzzled.

"I have told you how .. grateful I am .. but there is nothing else I can do to show my gratitude .. except try to .. please you."

There was a little silence. Then the Marquis said:

"Suppose I tell you that I prefer to have a quite normal marriage, as I envisaged with Caroline, in which you are my wife not only in name, but in fact?"

Because what he said upset her Rocana rose to her feet and walked across the room to the window.

The curtains had been drawn except over a French window which opened out into the garden.

She stood looking out. The light was fading from the sky and the stars were coming out, one by one.

It was very quiet and there was a faint breeze rustling the leaves of the trees.

It seemed to Rocana to have the magic she had always sought and found in beautiful places, a magic which was part of herself, her instincts, her dreams and her longing for happiness.

She felt as if she was reaching out blindly towards something that eluded her; something that she was afraid she would never capture.

Yet every nerve in her body and every part of her mind longed for it.

Then she started as she realised that without her hearing him the Marquis had risen too, and was standing just behind her.

"Are you thinking of running away from me?" he asked in a deep voice.

"I have . . nowhere to run . . to."

"Then I suggest you stay," he said, "and we will start with my horses and pictures and see where they take us before I do anything that might frighten you."

Rocana turned to look up at him.

"Do you mean that . . do you really mean . . it?" she asked.

Now her eyes were shining with the starlight, and the fear had gone from their depths.

"I do not often allow my decisions to be overruled," the Marquis said dryly, "but you are very convincing, Rocana, not only in what you say, but what you think."

"Are you . . telling me that you can . . read my thoughts?"

"Your eyes are very expressive."

"I am glad if they persuade you that I am right."

"I am not saying you are right," the Marquis contradicted "but merely that I will agree to what you want."

"Then . . thank you . . I am very grateful."

As if the subject was closed the Marquis then started to talk about what they would do tomorrow, and it was nearly midnight when Rocana said:

"I think I should go to bed . . There are so many . .

exciting things that I can talk to you about that I want to have all .. my wits about me."

"I take that as a compliment," the Marquis replied. "Go to bed now and, if you wish, join me when I ride in the Bois at eight o'clock."

"May I .. really do that?"

"I shall look forward to your company."

"Thank you .. thank you!" Rocana exclaimed. "I promise not to be late."

She rose from where she had been sitting to hold out her hand, wondering as she did so if it was the right way to say goodnight.

To her relief the Marquis took it, raised it perfunctorily to his lips in French fashion, and said:

"Go to bed, Rocana, and stop worrying. If you leave everything to me, I will try to make you very much happier than you have been in the past."

She smiled at him before she said:

"Now I am quite certain I am dreaming. I had half-expected that tonight I should have to sleep in the street .. or beg my way back to England!"

She spoke half-seriously, half-jokingly, and the Marquis said:

"I believe impersonators and forgers in France are taken to the Bastile."

"Then I am very grateful for the comfortable bed which is waiting for me upstairs," Rocana smiled. "Goodnight, My Lord."

She curtsied and walked towards the door which the Marquis opened for her.

She looked up at him as she stepped out into the passage and thought there was a strange expression in his eyes which she did not understand.

Then because she was relieved, excited and somewhat bewildered all at the same time, she ran upstairs.

Marie was waiting for her, to help her undress and get into bed.

. . . .

The following evening as she changed for dinner Rocana thought she had never had a more thrilling or delightful day.

For nearly two years she had crept about the Castle like a ghost, hoping not to be seen, because if she was, she would undoubtedly be reprimanded by the Duchess.

She had never been able to have a conversation with any outsider, or be listened to if she spoke to anybody except Caroline, so it was a joy beyond words to be with a man like the Marquis.

He was so intelligent, so well read, that she forgot to be frightened of him and found herself making sparkling replies to everything they talked about because he stimulated her imagination.

They rode in the Bois, and Rocana had found two extremely attractive summer habits among Caroline's clothes which the Duchess had bought for her trousseau.

One was in the pale blue of Caroline's eyes, the other a leaf green trimmed in Military fashion with white braid that Rocana thought was the smartest outfit she had ever seen and there was a black riding-hat to go with it, trimmed with a green gauze veil.

When she joined the Marquis at exactly eight o'clock she thought there was a glint of admiration in his eyes, although she could not be sure.

"For a woman you are surprisingly punctual," he said in his dry, mocking voice.

"As your wife, would I dare to be anything else?" Rocana replied. "And as a friend I did not wish to keep you waiting."

He smiled at her quickness.

Then instead of allowing a groom to help her he lifted her into the saddle and arranged her skirt over the pummel with an experienced hand.

The horse she was riding was not as magnificent as Vulcan, but nevertheless a fine and well-bred animal.

Rocana was completely unaware that she and the Marquis together created quite a sensation amongst the other riders in the Bois.

Most of them were men, and several greeted the Marquis as old friends and were obviously anxious to be introduced to his wife.

Because Rocana spoke to them in their own language they all exclaimed at her proficiency and her perfect accent.

Only when they were alone did she ask:

"Am I to say that my mother was French? Or should I let them go on believing I am Caroline?"

"I think for the moment we should leave things as they are," the Marquis replied. "Explanations are always a mistake, and my marriage will have been reported by the Duke in 'The London Gazette' as well as 'The Times' and 'The Morning Post'."

"I can see it is a complicated situation for you," Rocana said, "and I think it would be wise to wait for as long as possible to give Caroline and Patrick time to have left England."

"They intended to go abroad?" the Marquis asked.

"I think they were coming to France," Rocana replied, "but Patrick had planned everything down to the last detail, so I cannot believe there was any real danger of their being apprehended at the last moment."

She was sure this was the truth.

At the same time there was a little note of fear in her voice because she had lived in the shadow of her Uncle's Ducal authority for so long that it was hard to believe that anybody could defy him and win.

"You are worrying again, Rocana," the Marquis said, "and I like you best when you are smiling."

"Then I will smile," Rocana replied.

After their ride the Marquis took her to an exhibition of pictures which left her breathless.

"Mama would have loved seeing these," she said. "She taught me so much about the French artists, and although I have seen reproductions of them, it is not the same as seeing the originals."

She thought her enthusiasm rather amused the Marquis.

Then they went to luncheon at a Restaurant in the Bois.

Driving in his Phaeton, the groom sitting up behind them, they once again attracted the attention of everybody who saw them.

The Marquis noticed how unselfconscious Rocana was, and that she did not notice the admiration in the Frenchmen's eyes, or the curiosity and envy in the women's.

The luncheon, which was delicious, was eaten at a table for two, under the trees.

Rocana talked of pictures and horses and the Marquis found himself answering innumerable questions he had never been asked before.

Once when he hesitated with his reply, Rocana asked quickly:

"Am I boring you and being a nuisance through being so inquisitive? You must tell me if I am."

"I assure you I am not bored," the Marquis answered.

"I am well aware of how ignorant I am about you and your whole life," Rocana said, "and although I will try to learn as quickly as possible, I am afraid you will have to teach me so many things that you may find it very tedious."

"If I do I will tell you so."

"I was just thinking," she went on, "how wonderful it is for me to be with somebody like you. It is like being with Papa, only more so!"

"I am flattered!" the Marquis said dryly.

"I am not disparaging Papa," Rocana explained. "He was very clever, very witty and insisted that I should be able to hold what he called 'intelligent conversation', but he really preferred talking to Mama, and if she was there I could not hold his attention."

She sighed before she ended:

"So you can understand how thrilling it is for me to have you all to . . myself, at least for the . . moment."

131

"Are you putting a time limit on it?" the Marquis enquired.

"Of course," Rocana replied. "I am afraid that not only will some lovely lady snatch you away, but you will vanish and I shall wake up!"

The Marquis laughed.

"The trouble with you is that you are far too imaginative," he said, "and goodness knows what trouble I shall find myself in! You have caused enough trouble for me already and I am just wondering what the future holds."

"I am only hoping," Rocana said quickly, "you will not find me very dull."

"I think that would be impossible!"

The way he spoke made it difficult for her to know if it was a compliment or a criticism.

· · · · · · ·

Now as Marie helped her into another beautiful gown, she told herself that she was so lucky that for the first time since her father died she was not only happy, but unafraid.

"He is not really . . frightening," she told herself.

At the same time she knew that if the Marquis was angry with her, as he had been last night, he had the power to make her feel as if her heart had stopped beating and it was impossible to breathe.

'I must just keep him laughing,' she thought, 'and amused by what I say.'

She sent up a little prayer to her father for help, knowing how he had always managed to raise the tempo of any party he attended.

He had also drawn people by his magic as he always said he had been drawn by her mother's.

"I want that magic!" Rocana murmured.

She hoped the Marquis would be aware of it and would continue to be as kind as he had been today.

"You look very beautiful, *Madame*!" Marie was saying.

She brought Rocana's thoughts back to herself and she looked at her reflection in the mirror.

She saw that Marie had dressed her in a gown of very soft pink which in a subtle manner accentuated the gold of her hair and the mysterious darkness of her eyes.

The gown was trimmed with pink carnations around the hem and the shoulders and Marie had procured some real pink carnations from the garden which matched and arranged them in her hair.

They made her look very young, and as she entered the Salon the Marquis thought she looked like Persephone coming back from the bowels of the earth to bring the first blush of spring to the world outside.

He watched her walk the length of the Salon towards him and knew that because she was so slight Rocana had a grace that most young women lacked.

It was entirely natural and unselfconscious with nothing artificial about it.

As she reached him he said:

"I thought after dinner, if it pleases you, I might take you to a party which friends of mine are giving and where there will be dancing."

"That would be very exciting!" Rocana cried. "I only hope I can dance well enough! I have danced the waltz with Papa, but of course I have never been to a Ball since I grew up."

The Marquis stared at her. Then he said with a smile:

"That is something else I must teach you."

"Do you mind?"

"Of course not! I shall enjoy it!"

Rocana hesitated. Then she said:

"Please . . as I feel . . embarrassed at being so ignorant . . could we first go somewhere to dance where there will only be strangers . . and not your friends?"

"I think that is a sensible idea," the Marquis agreed, "and that is what we will do."

"You *do* understand!" she exclaimed.

"Did you expect me to be utterly obtuse, or should I say 'thick-skinned'?"

"No, of course not! It is only that you are very much more understanding than I thought you could possibly be, and I think you have an instinct about people's feelings that I did not expect."

The Marquis did not answer and Rocana went on:

"I think very few people have that particular instinct, but it is something Papa thought was magic."

"The magic you used on *Vulcan?*" the Marquis asked.

"Exactly!" Rocana agreed. "And it works on both animals and humans."

"Then I am delighted you should think I have it."

She smiled at him but before he could say any more dinner was announced and they went into the Dining-Room.

The meal was even more delicious than that of the night before.

Because Rocana was hungry she tasted everything she was offered, and drank a little champagne which the Marquis told her came from a vineyard he was thinking of buying.

"It would be very exciting to have your own vines," she said. "Could we go and see them?"

"I was thinking I would like to do that," the Marquis replied, "and my plan was to drive there as soon as we are tired of Paris."

"But not too soon," Rocana pleaded. "There is so much more I want to see in Paris, and I am sure there are many, many more pictures for you to inspect."

The Marquis was just about to reply when suddenly the door burst open and the noise of it made Rocana turn her head.

A man came into the room in an aggressive manner which seemed extraordinary.

Then as Rocana saw several servants behind him looking anxious, she realised he had thrust his way into the house and had not waited to be announced.

He slammed the door shut behind him, then walked across the room, his eyes on the Marquis.

"I heard you were here, My Lord," he said, "and if you thought to escape me, you made a mistake!"

He was speaking in English but with a distinct accent that was not French but showed, Rocana thought, he was either Austrian or from one of the Balkan countries.

He had a flamboyant look, with a curling moustache and clothes that while expensive and smart looked very un-English.

He advanced until he was standing only a few feet away from the Marquis before he went on:

"I consider your behaviour with The Princess an insult to me as a man, and I intend to take my revenge!"

The Marquis slowly rose to his feet.

"I must welcome Your Highness, to my house," he said in a very controlled voice, "and may I have the honour of presenting my wife."

Because she felt she should do so, Rocana also rose ready to curtsy as soon as the Prince looked in her direction.

Instead he was glaring in a very menacing way at the Marquis, and he retorted in a voice of barely repressed anger:

"If you think you can trick me by getting married and leaving England, you are very much mistaken! I am not a fool, Quorn, and I am well aware of the outrageous way in which you have been behaving and I have no intention of allowing you to evade your just deserts!"

"I can only regret that Your Highness should feel this way. . ." the Marquis began.

"You have insulted me," the Prince roared, "and you shall pay for it!"

Still very quietly, the Marquis replied:

"In which case, Your Highness, as I cannot refuse such a challenge, I will meet you at dawn."

Rocana knew this meant a duel, and as she looked at the furious anger on the Prince's face she made a little murmur of dissent, thinking how dangerous he might be in his desire to hurt the Marquis.

"Dawn be damned!" the Prince exclaimed furiously. "I am not going to fight you with pistols! I know your reputation as a shot, and I have a much better way of avenging myself from which you will not escape."

As he spoke he drew back the cape he was wearing over his evening-dress, and as he did so Rocana saw that in his hand he was holding a stick.

It flashed through her mind that he was going to strike the Marquis with it.

Then he must have pressed a secret catch for the casing fell to the floor, and now the Prince was holding in his hand a sword-stick, long and sharp, which glinted evilly in the light from the candelabrum.

He pointed it at the Marquis and said:

"Only when you die, as I intend you to do, My Lord Marquis, will I be avenged and justice be done."

As he spoke he drew back his arm and lunged forward, intending to pierce the Marquis with the sharp point of the rapier in his heart.

Without thinking, without hesitating, Rocana flung herself between the two men.

"You cannot kill an unarmed m. . .!" she began.

Then as her voice seemed to ring out, the words ended in a scream.

Her action had taken the Prince by surprise, and it was too late for him to lower his weapon.

Instead the point of the deadly rapier pierced the top of Rocana's arm at exactly the height if she had not thrown herself forward, that it would have entered the Marquis's chest.

Then as she collapsed onto the floor the Marquis moved for the first time since the Prince had attacked him.

He hit him hard on the point of the chin with the strength and timing of the experienced pugilist.

As the Prince fell backwards onto the polished floor, the Marquis picked him up in his arms and flung him through the half open window out into the garden.

Then as he fell followed by the shattered glass the Marquis without watching turned and knelt down beside Rocana.

. . . .

It seemed to Rocana that she was coming back on wave upon wave of darkness towards a very faint light.

Far away, as if from another world, she heard a voice say:

"Drink this!"

It was too much effort to disobey and she could feel the rim of a glass against her lips and a liquid tipped into her mouth and trickling down her throat.

It was strong and fiery, and although she tried to turn her head and refuse it the voice said again:

"Drink! It will make you feel better!"

"She's coming round, M'Lord," she heard another voice remark. "Her Ladyship's only fainted."

Then some of the darkness faded and Rocana could feel a burning sensation in her breast.

For some reason she could not understand she did not want to open her eyes, and she was afraid.

Then the Marquis's voice with a note in it that was different from what she had ever heard before said:

"Wake up, Rocana, wake up!"

Because she felt she had to do what he said, she opened her eyes, and found he was bending over her, his face near to hers.

For a moment it was hard to focus her eyes. Then she asked:

"Are . . you . . all . . right?"

"I am all right, thanks to you. And now I am going to carry you upstairs. The Doctor will be here as quickly as possible."

"The . . Doctor?" Rocana murmured.

Then she remembered what had happened.

She thought she gave a little cry, but it was little

more than a murmur, and she asked again:

"You are . . all right?"

"You were the only person he hurt," the Marquis said quietly.

He lifted her very gently up in his arms and as he did so Rocana had a quick glimpse of a crimson stain on her chest.

Then she was aware that her shoulder was covered with napkins from the dining-room table.

She wanted to ask questions and to know how badly she was wounded.

Then it somehow did not seem to matter and the strength of the Marquis's arms was very comforting.

. . . .

It was many hours later before Rocana could think clearly.

She awoke from a sleep which she knew had been induced by something the Doctor had given her to drink, and which had rendered her unconscious while he examined her shoulder.

She was now aware that she was in her own bed and her arm which had been properly bandaged was in a sling. She was wearing a nightgown, although she had no recollection of being undressed.

It suddenly struck her that perhaps the wound the Prince had inflicted on her might result in the loss of her arm.

She gave a little cry and as she did so there was somebody beside her, and she thought it must be Marie.

Still without opening her eyes she asked in a whisper:

"They . . they will not . . take my arm . . off?"

"No, no, of course not!"

It was the Marquis who replied, and as she opened her eyes she found him bending over her.

She was so surprised to see him because she realised the only light in the room was from a candle by the bed.

138

She could see the white frill of his night-shirt above the velvet robe he was wearing, and knew it must be night and he should be asleep.

"You only have a flesh wound," the Marquis said quickly, "although it will hurt you and be uncomfortable. I am very grateful to you, Rocana, for saving my life."

"He . . intended to . . kill you!"

"He is mad!" the Marquis said. "If it is any satisfaction to you, he will be suffering far worse than you are, and I hope it cools him down, the hot-blooded fool!"

The way the Marquis spoke made Rocana want to laugh, but it was too much effort.

Whatever the Doctor had given her made her feel rather stupid and as if her brain was filled with cotton-wool.

"I . . I am . . glad I . . saved . . you. . ." she said weakly and fell asleep.

. . . .

When Rocana woke again it was morning and Marie was tidying the room.

The sun was coming through the window and there was a huge basket of white orchids beside her bed.

"Are you awake, *Madame*?" Marie asked. "I am sure you would like me to tidy you, wash your face, and bring you something to eat."

"I . . I am . . thirsty."

Marie brought her a cool drink of limes which was sweet with honey and refreshing.

As her mouth was dry Rocana drank thirstily, then was aware that her shoulder was hurting her.

Marie knew by the expression on her face what she was feeling and she said:

"The Doctor will be here later to change your bandages, *Madame*. He will be very pleased that you have slept so well."

"I am still . . sleepy."

Rocana knew it was the drugs, or whatever he had

139

given her, which made her want to slip away again into oblivion.

Marie however insisted on washing her face and hands and arranging her hair.

It was still dressed in the elegant curls in which she had worn it last night, and Marie brushed it so that it fell on either side of her face nearly to her waist.

She tied it with little bows of blue ribbon which matched the curtains on the bed.

The Doctor came and after he had examined her wound, telling Rocana to look in the opposite direction he said in the way that only a Frenchman could have done:

"Because you are very beautiful, *Madame la Marquise*, and also very strong and healthy, your wound will heal quickly, and I do not think you will have a fever."

"Will it leave a . . very ugly . . scar?"

"I think not," the Doctor replied, "and anyway, it will only be a tiny white mark on the perfection of your skin which your husband will consider a decoration for bravery!"

This was a way in which she knew no English Doctor would have spoken, and she smiled at the bearded Frenchman as he kissed her hand and said:

"You are very brave, *Madame*, and I am very honoured to be allowed to treat anybody so lovely!"

When he had gone the Marquis, as Rocana hoped he would, came to see her and Marie left the room.

The Marquis looked down at her. Then he sat on the side of the bed and took her hand in his.

"How are you feeling?"

"All right . . thank you . . and the Doctor tells me the . . scar will not be . . very ugly."

"How could you have done anything so brave?" the Marquis asked in a strange voice.

"I . . I did not . . think what I was . . doing," Rocana replied. "I only knew it was . . wrong of the Prince to attack you. When you were unarmed."

140

"If you had not interfered his sword-stick would undoubtedly have pierced me in the heart," the Marquis said.

His fingers tightened on hers as he added:

"I was wondering how I could prevent him from killing me when you saved me!"

"I am .. glad .. so very .. very glad I did so. How could you .. of all people .. die like .. that?"

"Am I so special?"

"Of course you are! You are so .. magnificent .. always the winner .. the victor! It would have been an .. ignominious death .. or a crippling injury which I .. cannot bear to think of!"

"I am very grateful," the Marquis said, "but I am curious, Rocana, why you should think like that."

"I .. I just wanted to .. save you," she said in a sleepy voice.

As she spoke she felt her eye-lids closing and although she wanted to go on talking to the Marquis she found herself slipping away into a softness of clouds that were no longer dark, but grey.

The last thing she remembered was that he was still holding her hand in his.

CHAPTER SEVEN

"I want to get up," Rocana said.

The Nun who was arranging flowers on her dressing-table turned her serene face to say:

"The Doctor has promised that you shall come downstairs this afternoon for a little while. Until then, *Madame*, you must rest."

"I am sick of resting."

Rocana spoke quietly to herself, not wishing to upset the Nun whom the Doctor had sent to nurse her.

There were two of them. One was with her at night which meant never again had she woken to find the Marquis attending to her, and the other nursed her during the day.

Despite the Doctor's optimism she had run a fever for two days, which had left her very weak.

But the wound was healing on her shoulder, she no longer had to wear her arm in a sling, and there was only a bandage to show what had happened.

She watched the Nun for a few minutes arranging the lovely flowers which were brought to her bedroom every morning. Then she asked:

"Where is *Monsieur*?"

"He has gone driving, *Madame*."

"Driving?"

"*Oui, Madame*, I saw him leave quite early and I thought how smart he looked driving two horses that were so well-bred."

Rocana opened her lips to ask a question, then with difficulty prevented herself from doing so.

142

She wanted to ask if the Marquis had been alone.

Then she was astonished at the strange feeling the thought evoked in her breast.

He may have been alone when he left the house, but doubtless he was not alone when he drove in the Bois, or wherever else he was going.

For a moment she found it impossible to believe that the idea of his driving some beautiful lady as he had driven her could evoke an agonizing sensation, which she thought, was even more painful than the wound in her arm had been.

Then she admitted to herself that it was jealousy.

She was jealous of any companion of the Marquis: jealous that because she could not accompany him he had somebody else to talk to, somebody else who would make him laugh.

"How can I . . possibly feel like . . this?" she asked and suddenly knew the answer as if it was written on the bedroom walls in letters of fire.

She loved him!

Of course she loved him. How could she have been so foolish as to think that her ridiculous idea that they should be friends would last for long?

She knew now she had loved him long before she met him, when she had listened to the stories that were whispered about him and which now were inspired by envy and jealousy but also by an undoubted admiration.

It was because, as she had thought herself, he was superhuman, a man who was different from every other man.

"I love him!" she told herself, and knew how hopeless it was.

Perhaps after vanquishing the Prince he was again seeing the beautiful red-headed, green-eyed Princess.

Alternatively, if that had been dismissed as too dangerous an adventure, there would doubtless be dozens of other women to take her place.

Every story she had heard about the Marquis in the

143

past and the women who had loved him so frantically that they had even killed themselves for him or died of a broken heart seemed to taunt her.

As she lay back against the pillows in the beautiful room with its painted ceiling she thought that without the Marquis she might just as well be sleeping in a garret for all the pleasure it gave her.

"I want to be with him, I want to talk to him," she murmured.

She felt as if the sun had ceased to shine and she was encompassed by the same darkness which had covered her when the Prince's sword-stick pierced her shoulder.

After luncheon while there was still no sign of the Marquis Marie came to help her out of bed.

She dressed her, amid cries of admiration from the Nun, in one of the prettiest gowns in Caroline's trousseau.

It was white, but decorated with row upon row of real lace and ribbons of the blue of the sky outside which still seemed to Rocana to be as dark as if it was raining.

When she was dressed the Nun said:

"I am now going to say goodbye, *Madame*."

"Goodbye?" Rocana asked in surprise.

"You no longer need my services and may I say it has been a great pleasure and a privilege to be with you."

Rocana thanked the Nun and because she had nothing else to give her insisted on her taking back to the Convent one of the baskets of orchids which stood in her bedroom.

The Nun was delighted to have something to share with the other Sisters and said they would all pray for her.

"We will pray for your happiness, *Madame*," she smiled, "and that one day God will bless your marriage with children as beautiful and handsome as you and *Monsieur!*"

Because Rocana thought it was something which

would never happen, she had difficulty in replying.

Finally, after the Nun had said goodbye, she let Marie put the finishing touches to her hair, then rose slowly to her feet.

"My legs feel as if they are made of jelly!" she exclaimed.

"That is how I thought you would feel," a voice said from the doorway.

She gave a start as the Marquis came further into the room.

He was looking, she thought, more magnificent than usual and she found herself staring at him.

She felt that because he was there the sunshine was flooding in through the windows and he seemed as he walked towards her to be enveloped in light.

He was smiling as he said:

"As unfortunately none of my horses are clever enough to climb the stairs, you must allow me to take their place and carry you down to the Salon."

Rocana felt her heart give a little leap of excitement before she managed to say:

"I . . I hope I will not be . . too heavy for you."

The Marquis did not reply. He merely picked her up in his arms and she felt herself quiver at the strength and comfort of them and because she was so close to him.

Now it was impossible to find anything to say and, although she wanted to ask him where he had been, now that he was back it did not seem to matter any more.

He carried her slowly and carefully down the stairs and once they had crossed the Hall he set her down outside the Salon and said:

"There is a surprise waiting for you inside."

"A surprise?"

"Somebody whom I think you will be glad to see!"

When Rocana realised they were not to be alone she felt not only disappointed but also annoyed.

There was however no time to reply for a footman

145

opened the door and there was nothing she could do but walk into the Salon.

There were two people at the far end of it and for a second Rocana could not look at them in her resentment at their being there.

But as a woman ran towards her she cried out:

"Caroline!"

Then Caroline's arms were round her and she was kissing her as she said:

"Rocana, it is wonderful to see you, and so very, very kind of the Marquis to bring us here."

'So that is where he went!' Rocana thought.

Suddenly she felt as if the whole room was alight with sunshine.

Then Patrick was kissing her cheek and they were both talking at once.

"How can we ever thank you?" "It is all due to you that we are here!" "Everything is so wonderful!"

"And .. you are married?" Rocana asked when she could make herself heard.

"Of course we are married!" Caroline replied. "Patrick had it all arranged. And, dearest Rocana, the Marquis has been telling us that he is quite sure that neither Mama nor Papa has the slightest idea of what has happened!"

"They will undoubtedly have a shock," Patrick chimed in, "but because your husband has promised to take all the blame upon himself, when we do go home there will be nothing to make Caroline afraid."

Rocana looked at the Marquis for an explanation, and he said in his dry voice with the little twist of his lips that she knew so well:

"I have said that I will speak to your Uncle first, and tell him that it was entirely my fault that he was deceived. I will tell him the story which you invented."

"Will you really do that?" Rocana asked.

"He has said he will," Caroline interposed before the Marquis could reply, "and we are so very, very grateful."

146

Then there was so much to talk about, so much to hear and Rocana could only think how lovely Caroline looked because she was so happy.

Caroline and Rocana drank tea, but the Marquis and Patrick preferred Champagne, and of course, they were talking about horses.

Then before Rocana had learnt half of what she wanted to know, Patrick looked at his watch.

"As we do not wish to miss our train," he said, "I am afraid we must leave."

"Where are you going?" Rocana asked.

"To Nice," Caroline answered. "Is it not exciting? And although we guessed you were in Paris, we would not have dared to call and see you if the Marquis had not found out where we were staying and brought us here."

She smiled at him as she added:

"You are so much nicer than I thought you were, that I feel I ought to apologise."

"That would embarrass me," the Marquis replied, "and I am only so glad that everything has turned out so well for us – all."

The two men went ahead into the Hall to see if the carriage which was to take them to the station was ready, and Caroline put her hand on Rocana's arm as she said in a low voice:

"You are all right, dearest? He has not been unkind to you?"

"No, of course not!" Rocana answered. "He has in fact, been very, very kind."

"He is not half as frightening as I thought he would be," Caroline said, "and he was so charming when he brought us here to see you."

"I wondered where he had gone," Rocana said remembering how painful her feelings had been.

"I want you to be as happy as Patrick and I are," Caroline said, "or at least very nearly! Being married is just like being in Heaven!"

Patrick called her from the Hall and she rose to her feet.

"Thank you, thank you, dearest Rocana," She said. "If it had not been for you I should have lost Patrick and just wanted to die!"

Rocana walked with her to where the Marquis and Patrick were waiting.

She watched them get into the carriage, Caroline waving through the open window as they drove away.

Rocana and the Marquis walked back to the Salon and as they did so she asked:

"How could you have thought of anything so kind as finding Caroline and Patrick and bringing them here to see me?"

"I did not want you to go on worrying about your Cousin," the Marquis answered, "and as I discovered they were staying at an Hotel in Chantilly I drove there this morning and insisted they came here before they caught their train to Nice."

"They are very . . very . . happy," Rocana said with a little sigh.

"That was what I thought," the Marquis agreed.

Rocana would have sat down on the sofa, but he said:

"You realise it is nearly five o'clock and if you are going to dine with me tonight, which I would like you to do, I think you ought to rest."

Rocana gave a little cry of protest.

"Oh, no! I do not want to leave you!"

"We are in France," the Marquis replied, "and *Cinq à Sept* is the time when every sensible Frenchman and woman rests so that they shall be at their sparkling best in the evening."

He did not wait for Rocana to reply but picked her up in his arms.

She wanted to tell him that she had no wish to return to her bedroom, but because he had said she could dine with him she thought it best to do what he desired.

Then as he carried her up the stairs and she was conscious once again of his arms and his closeness, she remembered her father had laughed about the French interpretation of *Cinq à Sept*.

He had been talking to her mother in the Library and had not realised she was listening.

"It is a French habit, my darling, which has much to commend it. The French say they are resting, which is a polite word for a *tête-à-tête*, an assignation and of course, making love."

Her mother laughed.

"And they actually set that special time apart for such things?"

"Can you imagine anything more sensible?" her father replied. "It is something I think I shall introduce into my house. And make quite certain that between the hours of five and seven we are not interrupted."

Her mother had laughed, but Rocana had known that when her parents went upstairs with their arms around each other they were going to 'rest' in the French fashion.

Now it flashed through her mind that perhaps because the Marquis was so insistent that she should rest he had an assignation with somebody else.

'After everything I have said to him . . he has no idea that I would . . mind,' she thought unhappily.

Then once again there was that stabbing pain of jealousy in her breast, and she wanted to hold onto him and beg him not to leave her.

When he set her down in her bedroom Marie was there and although she looked at him beseechingly her pride prevented her from asking him to stay.

"I am pressing your prettiest negligée for you to wear tonight, *Madame*," Marie was saying. "Monsieur has ordered dinner in the Boudoir."

"In the Boudoir!" Rocana exclaimed.

"To save you going downstairs and having to dress-up as *Monsieur* put it," Marie explained. "But I am going now to order some special flowers from the garden for you to wear in your hair."

"Thank you," Rocana replied.

She thought as she got into bed that whatever she wore the Marquis would not notice.

149

Doubtless at this moment he was driving to call on some exquisitely beautiful lady who would be waiting for him in her *Boudoir*.

He would find her so attractive that he would hold her in his arms and kiss her in the way her father had kissed her mother as if she was infinitely precious.

"That is .. something he will never .. feel about .. me," Rocana told herself.

Because she felt so lonely tears came into her eyes and ran down her cheeks.

She did not attempt to wipe them away.

She merely lay thinking that the love she had for the Marquis was more agonising than any other pain which could be inflicted on her.

Then surprisingly the door which led into the *Boudoir* opened and he came into the room.

Because her eyes were filled with tears she could only feel he was there and could not see him very clearly.

He came towards the bed and sat down on the side of it facing her, and it was all so unexpected that she felt herself tremble.

At the same time she was vividly conscious of the vibrations and magnetism which came from him and were over-powering.

"You are not crying, Rocana?" the Marquis asked in his deep voice. "Are you in pain?"

"N. no."

"Then what has made you unhappy?"

She did not mean to tell him, but somehow because he was waiting for her answer she found herself saying:

"I thought you had .. left me .. alone."

"You had said you wanted to stay with me," the Marquis said quietly, "and so I thought it would be a good idea if we rested together."

Because of the way he spoke and because he was so near Rocana felt her heart turn several somersaults in her breast.

The pain had gone and there was a strange excitement seeping through her as if the sunshine was moving inside her body.

The Marquis took a soft linen handkerchief from his pocket and very gently wiped the tears away from Rocana's cheeks and eyes.

It made her tremble and now that she could see him clearly she realised that he too had undressed.

He did not speak but went round to the other side of the bed and taking off his robe got in between the sheets and lay back against the pillows.

Rocana gave a little gasp but he had left a gap between them. Although she wanted to look at him, she felt shy.

"Now what shall we talk about?" the Marquis asked. "Oh, yes, of course! Pictures and horses in which you know we are both interested, but I feel there is something else we should discuss first."

"What is . . that?"

"You have not yet told me why you were brave enough to save my life."

She did not answer and he said:

"I do not think any other woman would have thought so quickly or been so amazingly brave."

Because there was a deep note and something very warm in his voice, Rocana felt herself quiver.

Then she said, and there was almost a frantic sound to her words:

"Suppose he . . tries again? Suppose he . . shoots or . . stabs you . . and you are unable to . . protect yourself?"

"It is something he will not do," the Marquis said confidently.

"H. how can you be . . sure?"

"The Prince has already left Paris and returned to his own country."

Rocana gave a sigh of relief.

"I am glad . . so very . . very glad."

"Why?"

The question took her by surprise, and now she turned to look at the Marquis enquiringly.

He seemed nearer than she had expected and for a moment she could think of nothing except how handsome he was, and that he was very close.

"I was asking you, Rocana," he said quietly, "why you are so glad that I am safe."

He paused before he added:

"When you saved me you made me think at first that perhaps I meant something special to you, and that if I had died by the Prince's hand you would have been upset."

"Of course I . . would have been . . upset!" Rocana replied. "How could I lose you when. . ."

She stopped, realising she had spoken without thinking, and that what she had been about to say would have been very revealing.

Then she gasped for the Marquis put out his arms and drew her close against him.

He moved her very gently so as not to hurt her shoulder and at his touch she felt a thrill run through her whole body and she quivered against his, but not with fear.

It was impossible to think or to speak, but only to feel the magnetism of him.

Because it was so exciting she turned her face against him, aware that she could feel the strength of his hands through the thin transparent nightgown she was wearing.

"You have not answered my question, Rocana," the Marquis said very softly.

"I . . I have forgotten what it . . was."

"Now you are not telling me the truth, and you promised you would always be frank with me."

Because she did not answer he put his fingers under her chin and very gently turned her face up to his.

His action made her feel once again thrill after thrill running through her and she felt that he must be aware of it.

Their faces were very close together and as he looked down into her eyes she thought there was an expression in his that she had never seen before.

"Now, tell me," he said, "tell me exactly and truthfully what you feel about me."

As if he mesmerized her by the magic she could feel pouring out of him to tell him the truth Rocana found herself whispering what she had never meant to say out loud:

"I .. I love you! I .. cannot .. help it .. but I .. love you!"

"As I love you!" the Marquis said, then his lips were on hers.

She knew then that this was what she was longing for and crying for, and wanting as she had never wanted anything in her whole life.

His kiss seemed to give her not only the sunshine, but the moon, the stars, all the magic she had found in everything beautiful and had known instinctively she would one day find it in love.

It was a magic which seemed to pour through her, making her feel as if the Marquis drew her very soul from her body and made it part of his.

His kiss was so wonderful, so perfect, that Rocana knew that like Caroline she had reached Heaven, and found the love that was not only human but part of God.

This was what she had prayed for, this was what she had thought she had lost for all time, and yet it was suddenly hers.

The Marquis set her lips free and as if she was bewildered by the sensations he had given her Rocana said, her words tumbling over each other:

"I love you .. I love you .. but I never thought you .. would love .. me!"

"I think I loved you from the first minute I saw you," the Marquis replied, "when you were so clever with *Vulcan* and afterwards when I left the Castle I kept thinking about you, and although I tried not to do so, your eyes haunted me."

"Is that . . true?"

"It is the truth," he said, "and I thought today when Caroline was here that my usual luck had not failed me, and by a sheer quirk of fate I had married the right person, instead of the wrong one."

"Can it . . really be . . true?" Rocana asked.

The Marquis smiled.

"I can see it is going to take me a long time to convince you that I am telling the truth, my darling. And I will start by kissing you again which I have been longing to do ever since you told me we could only be friends."

"How . . could I have been so . . foolish?"

Then the Marquis was kissing her demandingly, possessively, passionately until as her whole body seemed to vibrate with the thrills he evoked in her, she pressed herself closer and still closer to him.

As her heart beat frantically against his she knew that she had excited him and he too was experiencing the magic sensations which rippled through her body.

Only when she felt as if he carried her into the sky and they had left the earth far behind did he say in a voice that she could hardly recognise:

"My darling! My sweet! I want you! God knows, I want you. But I would not do anything to frighten you."

"I . . am not . . frightened."

"Do you mean that? You are quite certain you mean that?" the Marquis asked.

There was a little note of passion in Rocana's voice he did not miss as she replied:

"Teach me about love . . please . . teach me to love you . . as you want to be . . loved."

"You are sure you are not frightened of me?"

"I am only . . frightened of . . doing something wrong."

He made a sound that was half a laugh, and half an expression of happiness.

Then he was kissing her once more, in a way that was even more possessive, more demanding than it had been before.

His hands were touching her and she knew they were both of them being carried away by a strange magic that seemed to leap up like a flame within them.

Although it was a fire, it was still mystic, spiritual and enchanting.

There was a light which was dazzling, a music which came from their hearts and as the Marquis made her his, she knew that this was the beauty that she had sought and which she had sensed in everything she saw.

The beauty of love, of life and of God, which could only be found when two people became one with the ecstasy and rapture which lifted them up into Heaven.

. . . .

A long time later, when the afternoon sun had gone and the room seemed as full of shadows as the garden outside, Rocana turned to kiss the Marquis's shoulder.

His arms around her tightened and he said:

"I have made you happy, my lovely darling? I have not hurt you?"

"I . . I did not know it was . . possible to be so . . utterly . . completely happy . . and at the same time . . not myself!"

"That is what I wanted you to feel my precious, and I think just now, we were neither of us human, but one with the gods."

"How can you be so wonderful?" Rocana asked. "Your magic is so strong that I know now that it is . . . love."

The Marquis gave a low laugh before he said:

"It is your magic, my adorable little wife, from which I have never been able to escape since I first met you. I felt it drawing me, holding me, and while I told myself I was imagining things, I know that you have cast a spell over me from which I can never escape."

"Supposing I . . bore you?"

"That would be impossible."

"H. how can you be sure?"

155

He pulled her a little closer before he said:

"You know it without my telling you that there have been many women in my life. But they have always disappointed me, and although I would not admit it, I was searching for something different: something I could not put into words, but which I knew at the back of my mind and in the depths of my heart."

It was as if he was telling her a fairy-story and Rocana looked up at him, her eyes very large and mysterious, and yet she understood exactly what he was saying.

"I was like a pilgrim," the Marquis went on, "who climbs a mountain that is on the horizon only to find there is another mountain and another horizon beyond that, and yet another.'

His tone changed as he added:

"I thought myself to be so self-sufficient, so complete in every way, that I would not listen to what you would call the 'magic' which told me that something was missing."

"But you were . . aware of it?"

"Of course I was aware of it," he replied, "and every time a woman disappointed me and the love I had expected to find was not there, I told myself cynically that I was expecting too much, and asking the impossible."

He sighed before he went on:

"Then I was back climbing another mountain in the hope that I would discover at the top of it the Holy Grail, the Golden Fleece, or to put it simply: the love which every man, if he is honest, searches for and believes that one day he will discover."

Rocana drew in her breath.

"And . . now?"

"I have found you."

"But . . suppose . . just suppose. . ."

He put his fingers over her lips.

"I have found you!" he said firmly. "You are everything for which I have been seeking, and thought was

156

just a figment of my imagination.''

He looked down at her face as if he was absorbing its beauty and continued:

"I adore your face, your eyes, your little straight nose and your lips which are different from any other woman's. When I touch them with mine I am aroused differently from any way I have ever been aroused before.''

"How is it . . different?''

"It is difficult to put into words,'' the Marquis answered, ''but while I desire you as a woman, and nobody, my precious, could be more desirable, I also want you in a thousand other ways.''

He kissed her forehead before he went on:

"Your brain stimulates me, and I find myself thinking over the conversations we have had with each other and longing to be talking to you again.''

It was what Rocana felt too and she gave a little murmur of delight as he went on:

"I know also that in some strange way your heart speaks to my heart and your soul to my soul. We have the same ideals, the same feelings, the same urge to help other people, to improve everything we touch and be generous with everything with which we are endowed.''

The Marquis gave a little laugh as he said:

"That sounds very serious, but, my precious, while you will be the most beautiful Marchioness of Quorn there has ever been, you are going to work very hard to improve a great number of different things, help those who need it, and inspire me.''

"I will love that,'' Rocana murmured.

"And of course, apart from all these things that always lay in the back of my mind,'' the Marquis went on, ''was the fact that the woman I made my wife would also be the right sort of person to be the mother of my children.''

He watched Rocana blush and said very softly and tenderly:

"I think my darling, that when we have children they will be handsome and beautiful and also endowed from the moment they are born with the right ideals."

Rocana hid her face against him before she said in a very small voice:

"Suppose I .. fail you? Suppose I am not .. good enough for .. you?"

The Marquis lifted her chin again so that he could look at her.

"What I am really saying," he said, "is that I am not good enough for you. But, darling, I am quite certain our magic will bring out the best in both of us."

"That is what I know it will do!" Rocana cried. "And because I love you I will try to do .. everything you .. want of me."

Because the way she spoke was so spontaneous and so sincere, the Marquis's lips found hers.

As he kissed her she felt once again rippling through her the strange fire that was love and magic and all the things he had said to her which were so beautiful.

They were not only part of their love, but an enchantment from which they could never escape.

Then as the Marquis's kisses grew more insistent and she could feel the magic that came from him intensifying as it joined with the magic that came from her, he was once again carrying her up into the sky.

Then as he made her his there was only the rapture, the ecstasy and the glory of their love which came from God, belonged to God, and was theirs for all eternity.

THE END

THE UNWANTED WEDDING
by Barbara Cartland

The tall, irresistibly attractive Duke of Tynemouth is angry and horrified at having to marry the young and innocent Honora.

However, when she is kidnapped on their wedding night, he suddenly realizes just how precious she has become to him.

0 552 12422 2   £1.25

JOURNEY TO A STAR
by Barbara Cartland

From Barbara Cartland, the world's top-selling authoress (Guinness Book of Records, 1984), comes the charming story of Tarina. A lovely but impoverished young girl, she agrees to act as lady's-maid to her cousin while on a trip to Siam. She does not foresee the devastating attraction that will grow between herself and her cousin's host, the glamorous and worldly-wise Marquis of Oakenshaw.

0 552 12397 8   £1.25

BARBARA CARTLAND TITLES AVAILABLE
FROM CORGI BOOKS

While every effort is made to keep prices low, it is sometimes necessary to increase prices at short notice. Corgi Books reserve the right to show new retail prices on covers which may differ from those previously advertised in the text or elsewhere.

The prices shown below were correct at the time of going to press.

ORDER FORM

All these books are available at your book shop or newsagent, or can be ordered direct from the publisher. Just tick the titles you want and fill in the form below.

CORGI BOOKS, Cash Sales Department, P.O. Box 11, Falmouth, Cornwall.

Please send cheque or postal order, no currency.

Please allow cost of book(s) plus the following for postage and packing:

U.K. Customers—Allow 45p for the first book, 20p for the second book and 14p for each additional book ordered, to a maximum charge of £1.63.

B.F.P.O. and Eire—Allow 45p for the first book, 20p for the second book plus 14p per copy for the next seven books, thereafter 8p per book.

Overseas Customers—Allow 75p for the first book and 21p per copy for each additional book.

NAME (Block Letters) ....

ADDRESS ....

....